THE THRILL CLUB

THE THRILL CLUB

EDWARD GREGORY CARROLL

CUTTING EDGE

ISBN-13: 978-1-957868-19-6

Published by
Cutting Edge Books
PO Box 8212
Calabasas, CA 91372
www.cuttingedgebooks.com

CHAPTER ONE

Captain Gil Baxter expertly eased the big DC-7 through the early evening fog and down onto the illuminated runway at Los Angeles International Airport, the ship responding certainly to his movements at the controls. For a moment the airplane skimmed the concrete, then the wheels touched, and they were down.

He nodded to Murphy, the co-pilot, to cut the two outside engines. They began taxiing to the Trans-U.S. hangar.

"Another one done," Murphy said, yawning. "I don't know what you're going to do, Gil boy, but I'm going to go home and go to bed."

"To sleep?" Gil grinned at him.

Murphy looked innocent. "Of course," he said. "What else?"

Gil shrugged. "How should I know? I'm just an innocent, oversexed bachelor. All my information comes out of books."

"Ha!" Murphy said.

"I thought you might be rubbing it in," Gil said. "Just because a goaty bastard like you can rush home and get rid of all his tensions doesn't mean that everyone can. Bragging about it is like eating cake in front of a hungry kid."

Murphy grew thoughtful. "Being married does have its pleasant moments," he admitted.

The plane was at a standstill now, and passengers were getting out of their seats and starting to file down the aisle. The stewardess, Carla O'Brien, was shooing them along toward the door. Murphy had swiveled in his seat and was looking at her.

"Of course, it's your own fault," he went on. 'You could probably have yourself a little wife of your own to go home to, if you really wanted to. Preferably an Irish colleen, since they make the best wives."

Gil grunted noncommitally. Murphy's buxom wife Helen thought it was a crime to be unmarried, and some of her enthusiasm had rubbed off on Murphy. Actually, Gil had given serious consideration to getting married. Except Brenda Hamilton was too busy social butterflying to consider matrimony.

"For goodness sakes, Gil," she'd said, with an impatient toss of her blonde head, "of course I want to get married and settle down and have children, but—"

Murphy's words cut into his thoughts: "Now, take Carla there."

Gil turned his thoughts and his gaze toward Carla, who at that moment was stooping to pick up an empty cigarette pack thrown into the aisle. Her blue skirt was busily straining against her rounded, very feminine behind. When she straightened, he regarded her legs, trim, curved, nylon-clad, functionally beautiful. Carla was a very pretty redhead with a slim but substantial figure, and he'd often admired her. A pity he wasn't in love with her instead of with Brenda.

He and Carla had some good times together in New York about two years ago. They'd been real buddies then. Carla was a native New Yorker, and she'd shown him the best eateries and drinkeries available on a co-pilot's pay. They'd had a good relationship, and it might have turned into something deeper—except just about that time Brenda Hamilton came along.

"You're missing a bet, Gil boy," Murphy was rambling on. "When you came in from a rough flight like this one, you could have a nice little wife waiting at home for you with a cold drink and maybe a hot suggestion for the evening's entertainment."

"I could," Gil admitted, "if I weren't too young to get married. They don't allow child grooms in this state."

"Too young?" Murphy said. "At thirty-two? Why you should have—"

Carla's voice broke in, "Are you two going to sit up here on the flight deck all night, gabbing like a couple of old women? I thought maybe one of you could buy me a drink to celebrate another safe landing."

She was standing in the doorway, trim, poised, looking very lovely and efficient in her uniform. Her flaming red hair was cut short to frame a wholesome, slightly freckled face. The jacket minimized her firm, rounded breasts, but Gil remembered how nice they were, how soft, how marvelously caressable. Quickly, he turned his thoughts from that direction.

"Happy to, babydoll," Murphy said enthusiastically. He got up to join her. "Just don't tell my wife. She's violently jealous. Coming, Gil?"

"Right with you two booze-hounds," he said, as briskly as he could manage.

But he was thinking about Brenda, where she was and what she was doing. He'd called her from Chicago, but there was no answer, and he wondered if she'd gone out on another of those 'trips' of hers. He didn't like it, but every time he'd brought up the subject Brenda snapped at him with a vengeance, telling him they weren't married yet and she had a life of her own to live and if he didn't like it ...

"Hey," Carla said, taking his arm, "surely the thought of having a drink with two buddies isn't that bad?"

He forced a grin at her. "Sorry. I was thinking dark, mysterious thoughts."

He noticed she more than held on to his arm as they made their way down the aisle. She squeezed it with a gentle pressure that was at once tender and reassuring. He glanced at her face, smiling inwardly at the tiny freckles gathered about her nose that he used to love to kiss in the days before Brenda.

"Brr," Murphy shivered as they came out of the airplane onto the ladder, "Me for some good old Irish coffee."

"Sounds good," Gil agreed.

"Booze for dinner," Carla said, shaking her head. "What a bunch of lushes."

The fog was sweeping the field, droplets of moisture hanging wetly in the air, making halos around the lights of the terminal. Gil glanced at his watch: six-forty-five. Too early for Brenda to have gone out for the evening. He'd finally given up any hope that she would be at the airport to meet him. He'd even suggested it a few times, but Brenda had dismissed it—nicely, but firmly.

Despite himself, he remembered what Carla had said once, "The unfortunate thing about love, Gil, is that sometimes it's not only blind, it's stupid!"

Gil was annoyed with himself for thinking of that. Brenda meant well. Her father had left her a good quantity of money, and it enabled her to travel within circles barred to peasants—like himself, he was forced to admit. But he couldn't make her give up her social pattern, any more than she could make him give up flying in favor of playing polo. Except this travel club bit of hers was more than annoyingly inconvenient; Gil couldn't give himself any valid reason why it disturbed him, only that it did. But after all, a man in love doesn't have to be rational all the time, does he?

They went into the neon-lighted flight office, closing the door against the dampness of the outside. The red-head behind the counter looked up and smiled expectantly at Gil. Her hair was longer than Carla's and much redder, and her face was thin and sensuous-looking. She was wearing a short, tight skirt, and a low-cut blouse.

"Rough one?" she asked.

"Bounced all the way," Gil answered. "Snow in Chicago, wind and rain over the Rockies, cross-wind over Arizona, fog in L.A."

"We'd already made arrangements for you to land at Burbank, in case the soup got too bad," the girl said. "By the way, your leave has been approved. All you have to do is sign these papers."

Gil sat down at the desk to sign the report and the leave papers, while the redhead bent over to show him where to sign. As she bent over, the low-cut blouse opened some more to show him to creamy-pink breasts cradled in a filmy bra.

The girl sighed. "You're a lucky guy," she murmured. "You're taking a vacation, and I have to work every night—until eleven o'clock."

"The curse of the working girl," Gil said sympathetically. He finished signing the papers, got up. "I put my phone number on the back of that leave paper, so you'll know where to find me."

"Fine. I'll take care of the flight report for you."

"Thanks," Gil said.

He was surprised to find that Murphy and Carla were no longer in the room. He found them outside, arguing.

"Take it easy," Murphy was saying. "Watch that Irish temper of yours, baby."

"Well, it makes me mad," Carla muttered. "I have to work until eleven o'clock," she mimicked. "The nerve of that female. Of all the cheap tricks! And an anatomy lesson thrown in for good measure!"

"Hey, what's going on here?" Gil said.

"Carla is making jealous-female noises," Murphy said.

"I'm not jealous," Carla snapped. "I just hate a cheap performance, that's all. She's not even a real redhead, either!"

Gil laughed. "You two can stop mother henning me. The young lady is quite attractive, but she's just not my type."

Carla opened her mouth to say something to that, but a sharp glance from Murphy silenced her. Gil knew what that was about. Carla had no great love for Brenda and didn't mind mentioning it. It reminded him that he had a phone call to make.

"Well, let's go get that drink," he said.

Carla linked arms with them, and Gil noticed that her touch was less personal this time. The brightly-lighted airline terminal was crowded, as usual; there are always people going somewhere, at all hours.

The street was alive with crawling cars as they walked to the FLIGHT DECK, several doors away. A softly-orchestrated version of a standard cascaded pleasantly over them as they entered the dimly-lighted bar and made their way to a booth.

"You two go ahead," Gil said. "Order me something nourishing. I'll be right back."

He turned away and threaded his way through the crowd toward the telephone booths. He closed the door on the crowd-noises and the music and dropped a dime in the slot. He dialed a familiar number, and the phone started ringing miles away, in Beverly Hills.

"Miss Hamilton's residence," a voice said. It was the maid, Carrie.

"Carrie, this is Gil Baxter. Is Miss Hamilton there?"

"No, she isn't, Mr. Baxter. She hasn't been in all day."

"We were supposed to have a date tonight," Gil said. "The flight ran into rough weather, and we got behind schedule a little. I tried to call her from Chicago. Do you know when she'll be back?"

"No, sir, she didn't say?"

"Did she say where she was going?"

Carrie hesitated.

"Is she at the country club?" he persisted.

"I ... I'm not supposed to say, Mr. Baxter, but ..."

"Then don't," Gil said. "I suspected she was out there anyway. If she comes in, tell her Gil Baxter called. She might remember the name!"

Angrily, he hung up. For a moment he stood staring at the phone, not seeing it. Brenda could be frustrating at the damnedest times! She knew he was coming in tonight, yet she goes wandering off with the country club set. He'd applied for a leave so that the two of them could spend more time together and finally get the business settled of whether or not they were going to get married. Sometimes, he wondered about her sense of values. Sometimes, he even wondered about his own.

He stomped back to the booth where Murphy and Carla were waiting for him, slid into the empty space beside her and stared glumly at the glass filled with icecubes and amber liquid.

"Scotch on the rocks," Carla explained. "I suspected you were going to call Brenda, so I made it a double."

Murphy stifled a smirk, but. Gil just said, "Thanks," and drank the liquid down without stopping.

"Wow," Carla said, not unpleased. "You do have a problem."

"Yeah," Gil said. "Look, I'm not going to be very good company, I'm afraid. Besides, I'm getting sort of pooped. I think I'll just run along. I'll see you people later."

"Sure," Carla said drily. "Keep in touch."

Ignoring her tone, Gil got up, reaching for his wallet.

"It's on me, buddy," Murphy said. "Give me a call in a couple of days, okay?"

"Okay. See you, Carla."

Without looking at her, he walked away and out into the street. He was waiting to cross over to the parking lot when he heard his name called. It was Murphy, a grim, unsmiling Murphy.

"We've been friends for a long time, Gil," Murphy said.

"Yes," Gil said, puzzled, "of course. But ..."

"During that time I've always thought you were a pretty great guy and for the most part I've tried to keep my nose out of your business." He hesitated, took a deep breath. 'You can take a swing at me if you like, but I think you're a fourteen-karat, grade-A idiot."

Gil sighed. "Now, look, Murphy ..."

Murphy shook his head impatiently. "No Gil, *you look.* Carla's a wonderful girl, and she's in love with you. *Why*, I don't know, but she is—for now, anyway. And you treat her like she doesn't exist, while you go chasing after some society tramp that ..."

Anger exploded in Gil with a suddenness that surprised him, and automatically he reached out and hit Murphy with a doubled fist. Even before the blow connected, he was sorry for the almost reflex action, but it was too late. His knuckles were stinging from the blow, while Murphy was recovering his balance, glaring more with pity than hatred.

"Murphy ..." Gil began, helplessly.

"Thanks, Gil," Murphy said calmly. "It makes things a lot easier. Carla needs a soft shoulder to lean on tonight, and you're practically forcing her into another man's arms."

Gil stared at him.

"All this talk about me and Helen is the bunk," Murphy went on. "I haven't gone to bed with her for over two months. She's living with her mother and planning on a divorce."

"Murphy, I'm sorry," Gil said. "I didn't know."

'Here's another thing maybe you didn't know," Murphy said, turning to go. "I'm going to make it with Carla, whether you like it or not!"

CHAPTER TWO

Gil stood in helpless frustration, staring at Murphy as the copilot went back into he FLIGHT DECK.

Gil shook his dead in bewilderment. Somehow, Murphy had seemed the happy, devoted husband, and on the few times he'd seen Helen, Gil thought she was very much in love with her husband.

He shrugged. Well, you never know. Maybe it would work out with Murphy and Carla. He hoped so. They were a couple of good kids. At least, he thought he hoped so, but he wasn't sure. He felt a twinge of uneasiness engulf him at the thought of losing Carla. Funny, it hadn't bothered him before.

Of course, before he hadn't been faced with the prospect of losing her. It annoyed him that he was jealous.

"You can't have every girl you know, Gil Baxter," he told himself, half-aloud. "You do have Brenda."

Brenda, over whom he had just slugged his best friend. His knuckles ached, and yet there was a deeper ache thinking about what he'd done. "**Society tramp**," Murphy had called her. Well, he was wrong. He didn't understand Brenda; he didn't really know her or understand her background, her motivations.

One thing was certain: Gil had problems of his own without worrying about Carla and Murphy. He had to settle a few things with Brenda, and one of the things was this business of the tourist club trips she insisted on taking. Her insistence on putting these uppermost had always bothered him, as did the trips themselves. He'd tried to convince himself that they were excursions of the idle rich, harmless meanderings that were of no concern.

Except Brenda was almost fanatical in her determination to go on them, and when she returned from them she seemed different. Different in a way he found difficult to describe.

He turned and walked out to the parking lot, nodding to the guard as he went past. The black Jaguar crouched where he'd left it, glistening with droplets of mist that had condensed on the metal. Gil unsnapped the tonneau cover, threw it in back. He got in, and beneath his prompting, the engine roared into life, growling happily.

Gil swung the car out of the lot and headed north, toward his Hollywood bachelor apartment. He thought of going into Beverly Hills to the plush mansion the late Hamiltons had willed to daughter Brenda, and just wait there until she arrived and then have it out with the girl. But if she'd gone on one of her trips, Brenda might not be back for days.

"Damn it!" he thought angrily. *"She knew I was getting a leave!"*

The blood started boiling in his veins, and he pulled into the nearest gas station that had a telephone booth. He looked up a number, dropped coins in the slot and dialed.

"Arroyo Country Club," a female voice said.

"I'd like to speak with Miss Brenda Hamilton, please."

"What is your name, please?"

Gil hesitated. "Gil Baxter," he said finally.

"Is she expecting your call, Mr. Baxter?"

"Yes," Gil lied.

"Hold on, please. I'll have her paged."

Gil held on. He stared through the glass windows of the telephone booth at the swirling fog—and wondered what Carla and

Murphy were doing now. He cut off that line of thinking right there. Whatever they were doing was their own business.

"Hello, Baxter," a male voice said.

"Yes," Gil said.

"This is Charlie Clark. You don't know me, but I heard the operator paging Brenda Hamilton, and all you'd have gotten was that she doesn't seem to be around. She's in a meeting right now."

"A meeting?"

"The tourist club is planning their next adventure into the unknown," Charlie Clark said wrily.

Gil laughed. "You don't sound like a devoted member."

"I'm not a member at all," Charlie Clark said "It's a very exclusive club."

"Too exclusive to be interrupted for a phone call?" Gil wanted to know.

"Not as far as I'm concerned. By the way, if you're ever out this way, drop in and I'll buy you a drink ... if you don't mind talking to an old man. Just tell the guard you're my guest."

"I'd like that."

"Meanwhile, I'll see if I can drag Miss Hamilton out of her den. If you don't hear from me in three days, send out the St. Bernards."

Gil waited, wondering why Charlie Clark wasn't a member of the club. Didn't he want to be, or wasn't he invited? In any event, he seemed like a nice guy, and it might be interesting talking to him—especially since he was at least closer to the tourist club and perhaps knew something about the organization.

"Gil?" It was Brenda's voice, annoyed.

"I'm glad to see you still remember me," Gil said.

She ignored his sarcasm. "I was in a meeting. Didn't Charlie Clark tell you?"

"He told me. I just thought our future might be a little more important than a club meeting. Did you forget I was getting a leave tonight?"

"Of course not." She sighed in exasperation. "But there's no sense in being melodramatic about it. After all, you've got ten days. We've got ten days. And this meeting is important. The tourist club is planing another trip."

"Where this time?"

"Can't tell. That's the beautiful part of the plan. We discuss it, but nobody really knows what's the program until we arrive. It makes it more exciting that way."

"I'll bet." Gil couldn't understand why a guided tour should make Brenda so expectant, but he didn't want to argue with her. "I hope you're not taking off for awhile. I'd like to see you for a long, uninterrupted time."

She hesitated. "The trip will be in a few days," she said.

Gil groaned. "Well, you're not going, of course."

"Gil ..." she began.

"For Pete's sake, Brenda." Gil exploded, "where's your sense of values. I'm the guy who loves you, remember? I've got ten days. If on insist on going on a trip, let's go on one ... together."

"Gil, I'd like to, but ..."

"But what?" Gil's voice was like ice.

"I do have certain obligations ..."

"But none to me, I suppose?"

"Gil, you don't understand. My social affairs are a part of my life. You can't just come in and disrupt them."

"Okay, let me join them, then."

"What?"

"Let me join the tourist club and go along with you into the wilds of wherever you're going. What's wrong with that?"

"Simply that you're not a member," Brenda explained, "and you can't become a member overnight."

"I know. Charlie Clark said it was a very exclusive club."

"If I were you, I'd stay away from Charlie Clark," Brenda advised. "He's a troublemaker and a busybody."

"Anyway, can I pick you up tonight?"

"I'm sorry, Gil, but I don't know how late I'll be. I'm pretty tired right now. I'd better go right home … I've got my own car here … and I'll call you tomorrow."

'Sure," Gil said. "You do that!"

Angrily, he slammed the receiver into its cradle. Brenda had given him the brushoff, but good. The part that hurt was the injury to his masculine vanity: she'd done it in favor of a tourist club. More and more his curiosity was being whetted by this club. He couldn't get any information out of Brenda, that was clear. "Don't see Charlie Clark," she'd told him. Well, he **would** see Charlie Clark, and maybe he could find out the answers to some questions that were irritating him.

He got back in the Jaguar and headed it toward Hollywood. The farther he got from the ocean, the more the fog dissipated, and by the time he reached his apartment on Lexington Avenue the air was only visibly damp. He pulled into the carport, walked up the steps, circled the lighted swimming pool, and entered his apartment.

He switched on the lights and the FM radio, and began pulling off his tie. Carla was probably in the arms of Murphy by this time, and Brenda was in the throes of a meeting to decide would this month take them to the sunshine of Acapulco or the skislopes of Sun Valley.

He thought of Carla—and of the last time they'd been together—really together, as only a man and a woman can be with each other. He smiled and sat down and let the memory some sweeping over him ...

It had been in New York, two years ago, and they were sitting on a couch in Carla's apartment, resting in each other's arms. The lights were turned low, the radio was on and playing softly, romantically. Outside, the frantic world of the big city was something that had ceased to exist. Gil felt relaxed and at peace with the world. He had his arm around Carla's waist and she was nestled snuggly against him with all the wonderful warm sweet femininity of her, and he nuzzled his face through the forest of her hair and planted a kiss on her cheek.

"Did I ever tell you you're wonderful?" he asked.

'Not lately," she said.

"You're wonderful," he said. "You give me guided tours, you sew on my buttons, you feed me. I'm beginning to wonder what other talents you have."

"You'd be surprised," she said, with a mysterious smile.

"Not me," he said, "I'm a jaded airline pilot, without a spark of romance in his soul. C'mere, I'll prove it!"

And he grabbed her gently and turned her and covered her lips with his and pulled her close to him. It started out to be a quick grateful kiss, but that wasn't the way it ended. He tried to pull away, but her arms went out around his neck and held him, and he lost interest in pulling away. She squirmed her body against his to a more comfortable position, and he found himself helping her, and then more than helping her. Their tongues were alive in each other's mouths, and their hands were moving in soft caresses.

When they came up for air, he said, "Lady, you're in danger of being seduced!"

She laughed. "Not a chance. **You're** the one that's in danger."

Then the laughter died as they looked at each other, studying each other's face, aware of the closeness of their bodies, the great fondness they held one for the other.

Carla turned away. "Gil ..."

Impatiently, he shook his head. He got up, scooping her into his arms with the same motion, and walked across the living room and kicked open the half-closed door of her bedroom. He lowered her carefully to the floor in the dimly lit room and stood before her. Her breasts were rising and falling as she breathed. He looked at her for a moment and then he reached out.

"Gil, oh Gill" she cried.

She put her arms around his neck and pulled him toward her, kissing him hungrily on the lips and the neck and the cheek, seeming to exult in the knowledge that his maleness was responding to her.

In the dimness they stood by the bed and undressed each other. There was no need to speak; their hands communicated all thoughts necessary for understanding, and then as they lay together on the bed their bodies took over.

For what might have been an hour they lay there, side by side, their bodies and hands and lips talking the silent language of love, exploring, discovering, exulting ...

Gil shook his head and brought himself forcefully to the world of the present—the world without Carla to love. But the memory of her was still with him, as well as the physical evidence her memory had erected in him—the rapidly beating heart, the expectant quickening of his pulse, the coming shortness of breath.

He thought about the redhead, then, the one in the Flight Office who had to work until eleven o'clock. He thought about those inviting pink creamy breasts of hers and the smile she'd given him and the way her clothes fit her. On impulse, he dropped into the chair beside the phone and dialed a number.

"Trans-U.S.," a voice said.

"Flight Office, please."

A pause, then a honey-liquid voice said, "Flight Office. Miss Sherwood speaking."

"This is Gil Baxter. Miss Sherwood," Gil said. "Are you the young lady I was talking with about my flight report?"

"Yes, I am. Is everything satisfactory?"

"No," Gil said. "Not yet, anyway. I'd like to have a talk with you. Sometime after eleven o'clock."

He could almost hear her smile over the phone. "Of course," she said.

"Shall I pick you up?"

"Let's meet somewhere. I notice you live in Hollywood. So do I. Why don't I stop off at your apartment, and we can take it from there."

"Fine. By the way, what's your first name?"

"Jan."

"I'll see you about eleven-thirty, Jan."

"Right … Gil. See you."

Gil hung up. He felt much better. It was pleasant talking to a girl who was just a girl and not a committee chairwoman. It would be pleasanter seeing Jan Sherwood. She was an attractive girl.

Whistling, Gil pulled off his uniform and headed into the bathroom, where he turned on the hot water in the shower. As the water played about his body, he felt his tenseness go down the drain with the gurgling water. If Brenda wanted to play games, then Gil Baxter could play games … with somebody else. Maybe that was Brenda's trouble: she was too sure of him. She thought she could stand him up on dates and go running off into the wilds any time she felt like it, without regard to his feelings. Well he'd show her!

He toweled his body dry with vigorous strokes, put on a bathrobe, lit a cigarette and went into the living room. The clock told him it was eight-fifteen. At least three hours before Jan showed up, just time enough to relax with a smoke before getting ready for whatever pleasures the evening had to offer.

He lay down on the couch, closed his eyes, inhaled deeply on the cigarette, and listened to the soft melodies coming from the radio. Funny, how tired he seemed all of a sudden. No not tired—sleepy. The warm shower must have done that. He stubbed out the cigarette on a nearby ashtray and closed his eyes again. Just for a few seconds ...

The front door chimes sounded, and Gil fought his way through layers of unconsciousness. He sat up on the edge of the couch, rubbing remnants of sleep from his eyes. The clock told him it was midnight now.

"Great!" he muttered. And he was still dressed in his bathrobe!

He got up and went to the door, opened it.

"Hi," Jan Sherwood said brightly.

"Hi," he said, thinking with misgivings how he must look to her, sleepy-eyed, hair rumpled, undressed. "Come in."

She walked in, and he closed the door behind her. She was still wearing the tight skirt, the low-cut blouse he'd admired in the Flight Office.

She smiled sensuously. "Do you always greet your female guests this way?" she said, indicating the robe.

Wakefulness came bursting upon him, and Gil noticed with embarrassment that the robe had fallen open in front. Hastily, he pulled it together and roped it more securely about him.

"Not always," he said, adding lamely, "I fell asleep. Would you care for a drink?"

"Love one."

He went to the bar while she sat on the couch and crossed her legs. They were smooth, trim legs, curved very nicely. She had a slim, rounded figure, and everything he'd seen and was seeing seemed inspiring and aesthetic.

"We have a little bit of everything," Gil announced. "What would you like."

"Something simple," she told him. "I feel like having an uncomplicated evening."

"I'm having a Scotch on the rocks," he said.

"Make it two, then." Jan stretched, and the skirt hiked up another inch above her knees. "Nice little place you have here."

"Thanks," Gil said, forcing his attention to pouring Scotch over rocks.

"That girl you were with today. Is she your girl friend?"

Gil came back to the couch with two drinks, handed her one. "She's my stewardess," he said. "We're just old friends."

"Buddies, probably," the girl said.

Gil grinned at her. "Probably. I'd better get some clothes on."

She caught his hand. "Captain Baxter," she said, teasingly, "you're not afraid I'll take advantage of you, are you?"

Her sensuous face was taunting him. Gil sat down beside her.

"As a matter of fact," he said, "I was sort of hoping you might."

Their thighs were just barely touching. Gil allowed his eyes the pleasure of roaming slowly along the length of her body, across the rounded breasts, the slim waist, down to the trim nylon-clad legs exposed several inches above the knee. He noticed her watching him, and she continued smiling that sensuous smile but made no movement to cover any exposed flesh. In fact, she even leaned forward so he could see more of the cleavage under the blouse.

"You like?" she said.

Gil nodded and sipped at his drink. He was beginning to feel tense again, but it was a tenseness of anticipation. Thoughts of any other woman seemed far away just then. He nearly jumped when she placed a tentative hand on his leg.

She laughed. "My, you're nervous."

"Lovely girls always make me nervous," Gild told her, placing his drink on the coffee table.

He took the drink from her unresisting hands and placed it beside his glass, and then he reached out and put his arms around her.

"Oh, Gil," she breathed.

She put her own arms around him the fingers, moving along his back. Her eyes half-lidded, her lips parted, her body moved expectantly.

Gil kissed her on the neck and along the ear and the cheek and then on the mouth with lips parted. His breath was becoming hoarse and ragged, and his heart was beating wildly. He could feel the movements of her rounded breasts again him, the gentle shifting of her hips.

She moaned in anticipation, and then suddenly she released him and stood up. Puzzled, Gil reached for her and then stopped as he realized what she was doing. She was smiling provocatively and licking her lips, and with slow, deliberate movements she started undoing the buttons of her blouse.

She pulled the blouse from her, let it drop to the floor, unzipped and quickly stepped out of the skirt. For a moment she stood like a slim, beautiful, wonderfully feminine statue in her bra, panties and stockings. Then she reached around in back of her to unhook the bra. In a second the bra had joined the pile of clothing on the floor and her creamy breasts were gloriously nude. She pulled the panties down over her thighs and stepped out of them.

Gil stared at her, fascinated, as she held out her arms to him. Then he got up quickly, scooped her into his arms and headed into the darkened bedroom. She was clinging to his neck, her lips working over his face. She was no statue. Her flesh was soft and responsive, and he could feel the blood pounding through his veins as he gently placed her on the bed and drew off his bathrobe and lay down beside her.

Arms tightened, mouths met with dancing tongues, bodies molded.

"Carla," Gil breathed, "Carla, my darling."

Suddenly, all motion stopped, and he realized what he'd said and felt cold with the knowledge. He opened his mouth to say something without knowing what he could say, but before he could, she laughed humorlessly and said, "You bastard! You know my name's Jan."

Before he could stop her, she removed her arms from him and sat at the edge of the bed. He reached for her, but she evaded him and stood up.

"Jan, wait. I'm sorry."

"Not as sorry as you will be," Jan promised. There was no hostility in her tone, only matter-of-factness. "Look, I don't mind going to bed with a guy I hardly know, but I like him to at least be aware that I'm the one he's with and not some other chick he wishes were with him."

"I knew it was you. I don't know what made me say that."

"Probably because you're in love with this girl—what's her name?—Carla. It doesn't matter. I'm out of the mood, anyway."

She walked back into the living room, where Gil could hear her pulling on her clothes. He got up and pulled on the bathrobe again. He'd been feeling sheepish, but now he began to feel sick with frustration. He stood in the doorway, wistfully watching her hook her bra.

"Look, I know your pride was hurt," he said. "So I said I was sorry, and I am. What more do you want?"

She smiled, but the smile had neither sensuality nor enthusiasm this time. "Let's face it, fly-boy. It was more than just a simple goof. I was thinking of this as an investment, because I like you. I though we might make it together, not merely for tonight, but for other nights, too." She sighed. "Except if your love for this other girl is that strong, I'd be wasting my time."

"Jan, at least stay for a drink."

"I'm not thirsty, but thanks anyway." She finished dressing, went to peck him sisterly on the cheek. "See you at the flight office sometime."

She opened the door and closed it behind her, firmly. He could hear her high heels clattering across the concrete patio and into silence.

Gil felt physically and emotionally sick. The memory of that soft female body returned to taunt and frustrate him, and he knew it could have been very nice. And yet he knew why he'd called out Carla's name. He was wishing it was Carla in his arms, instead of Jan.

He went to the bar to get himself a drink, and paused only long enough to consider something that suddenly occurred to him: funny, he hadn't even thought of Brenda.

CHAPTER THREE

It was twelve-thirty in the morning, and Gil stood in the center of his apartment, the bathrobe corded loosely around him, knowing it would be impossible to sleep. The redhead Jan had gotten him worked up to a fever pitch and then put her clothes back on and walked off in a huff. He could understand how she felt; her feminine pride had been hurt. But he also knew how **he** felt, and the frustrated longing inside him was almost painful.

He went to the phone and dialed Brenda's number. After a half dozen hings, the maid Carrie answered, sleepily.

"This is Gil Baxter, Carrie," he said. "Sorry to wake you. Is Miss Hamilton there?"

"Yes, she is, Mr. Baxter," Carrie answered patiently. "She came in about an hour ago. But I think she's asleep."

Gil hesitated. There were so many things he had to talk over with Brenda, so many things. The Past. The Present. And most important of all, the Future. The future not only of the two of them but of their baby.

Brenda had told him quite casually, the day before his flight.

'Darling, guess what?" she'd said. "I'm pregnant."

He stared at her for a moment, not fully comprehending. "Marvelous," he said finally. "We can get married right away."

She laughed. "Dont' be silly, Gil darling. I'm not that pregnant. It's not as though we have to have a shotgun wedding, you know. I thought about having an abortion—it would be easy, I've got the money and some friends who know a doctor; oh, it would be all very safe—but it's your baby, Gil, and I want to have it."

For some reason, Gil didn't feel like a trapped male. He loved Brenda, and he loved her more because she was pregnant hy him and wanted to have his baby. They had been fully intimate on only several occasions—but all it took was once, he reminded himself—aand the thought of her magnificent golden body made his maleness ache the more for her.

"Mister Baxter," Carrie's voice interrupted his reminiscence, "are you still there?"

"Carrie, would you check to see if Miss Hamilton is awake. If she isn't, don't disturb her, but if she is, I'd like to talk to her."

Carrie went away, and a few minutes later Brenda's voice came over the phone.

"Gil? Gil, is that you? What in the world are you calling up at this hour for?"

"I'm lonesome," Gil said. "I want to see you."

"Fine. I want to see you, too. Tomorrow."

Gil wet his lips. "I needed you, Brenda."

"Do you mean emotionally or physically?"

"Both."

She laughed. "That's very flattering, Gil, but really I can't come running to you every time you get a ..."

"It's more than that, and you know it," he said, hastily. 'We've got a lot to talk about.

"I know that. Gil, I love you, but right now I'm very tired and I'd like to get some sleep. Why don't you call me tomorrow?"

"Sure," Gil said. "If you don't have any social butter-flying to do, and maybe someday we'll get married if your Goddam Tourist Club hasn't scheduled a trip for the same day!"

She hung up, and for a moment Gil held the receiver in his hand, reluctant to admit that the connection had been severed.

Then he replaced the receiver in its cradle and went to fix himself a drink. He poured a lot of Scotch into a glass and went with it to the couch and lay down.

He wondered if he'd have called out Carla's name when he and Brenda had gotten together. It was a strange thought and one which he now had no chance of finding out about. Brenda was going to bed alone tonight. But was Carla? Or would sweet, lovable, innocent Murphy see to it that she wouldn't be lonely?

He was sorry for that last thought and he drank deeply from the Scotch in an effort to forget. But he couldn't forget the fire that was burning way down deep inside him, unquenched and insistent. He drained the last few drops of liquid from his glass and got up. Maybe a shower would relax him.

He'd gotten off his bathrobe and was in the bedroom when a sudden thought came. There was a bar just a few blocks away, a friendly neighborhood type place. Perhaps a couple of beers, some conversation, a little fresh air would help.

He dressed in sportshirt, slacks and sportcoat, and went out. The patio was damp and mist hovered eerily above the lighted swimming pool. A few lights in adjoining apartments were lit. The air was cool and damp, but it was clear. The streets were empty, except for an occasional car hurrying past.

The Green Room was not as lively as he'd hoped. Several people were seated at one end of the bar farthest from the door. At the far end, beneath the glare of a bare bulb, two men were playing shuffleboard. On the jukebox, Sinatra was crooning the miseries of unrequited love, softly, sadly, without regret.

Gil climbed on a stool near the door. The bartender came up, nodding.

"Double scotch," Gil told him.

As the bartender moved away, Gil looked down the length of the bar and was startled to see a young girl sitting a half-dozen stools away. Apparently, she had just come in. She was watching him, and he wondered why. She had long black hair which cascaded down about her shoulders, but he couldn't make out her features in the dim light.

She got off her stool and moved down the bar toward him. Gil watched the way she walked—like a girl in a tight dress ought to walk—and he felt the fires of his body again.

She hesitated, then smiled apologetically. "Sorry. I thought you were someone I knew."

She turned slowly, but Gil reached out impulsively and caught her arm. She didn't resist.

"I could be someone you know—if you'd let me introduce myself. Can I buy you a drink?"

She hesitated.

"Are you alone?"

"Yes," she said. She smiled again and climbed onto the stool beside him. "At least I was. I'd like a brandy and soda. "

He ordered her one and then said, "My name's Gil Baxter."

"Glad to meet you, Gil," she said. "My name's Laura."

Gil felt a warm glow pervade him. It was due partly to the amount of alcohol he'd consumed, which was just beginning to catch up with him. But it was very nice sitting there, drinking casually, talking, with a girl he could relax with and not worry about offending. A girl, he noticed, whose thigh was pressing against his and whose hand had somehow casually come to rest in his lap.

In the neon-lit world of the bar, Laura's thin features held an almost mystical quality that took what prettiness her face had and enhanced it. Her breasts were quite large, and she made a point of thrusting them proudly at him, rubbing them enticingly along his arms in a casual gesture that could even have been accidental.

But it wasn't accidental. Gil knew that. None of her move-ments were. They were calculated to show what a desirable female she was, and to convey promises of more to come.

Her hand moved along his leg, her breast along his arm, and she placed her head against his shoulder so he could smell the perfume of her black hair.

"Tell you what, Laura," Gil said, trying to sound casual. "I live just a few blocks from here. Why not come over to my place for a couple of drinks?"

"I'd like that," she said softly.

He slid off his stool, surprised that he felt so unsteady.

"Are you all right, Gil?" she asked. She took his arm. "Here, let me help you."

"Thanks. Guess I drank more than I thought."

They went into the street. The cool air swept around them. The streets were empty and dark. The sound of their footsteps were load in the silence. She gripped his arm tightly as they walked down the street.

The cold air was beginning to wake Gil, but he still felt groggy. But he had no intention of passing out. Not with a willing young lady hanging onto him. The needs of the flesh are frequent and insistent, and if he couldn't have the one he wanted he would have Laura.

"Much farther?" she wanted to know. She shivered against him.

"Another block," he said, and then he heard the soft whisper of footsteps behind him.

He tried to turn, but Laura had a firm grip on his arm. All he could do was duck instinctively. A hard object raked the back of his head, causing pain and darkness. Laura released him, and he felt himself falling heavily to the concrete sidewalk.

Rough hands fumbled at his clothing, reaching for his wallet, finding it. The bright lights of a car flashed over him, the screech of brakes was loud in his ears.

"Let's get out of here, " a man shouted.

There was the clatter of heels running.

"Gil." A familiar feminine voice. "Gil, are you all right?"

Someone was trying to turn him over. The pavement was hard and cold, and there was an intense pain in his skull. He forced open his eyes.

"Carla," he said, "what ...?"

She shook her head impatiently. "Explanations later. Right now, how do you feel?"

"Not bad. I rolled with the blow." A sudden thought: "Where's Laura?"

"The girl? She went with them. You sure pick some fine companions. Maybe I should stick around more often to see that nothing happens to you."

"Maybe you should," Gil said.

Then he remembered Brenda, whom he loved and who was the mother of his child. It wasn't fair to Carla, even to joke about a permanent relationship.

With Carla's help, he rose to his feet. Her M.G., motor running, lights burning, was parked beside the curb with the door open. He got in, slumped against the cushion. Carla got in the other side, drove in silence to his apartment.

"I feel a little shakey," he apologized. "I did a little drinking earlier, and the blow on the head didn't help any. You'd better help guide me past the swimming pool."

She nodded and helped him from the car. He had his arm around her shoulders, and her arm was around his waist, and there was nothing sexual about the embrace, but still it was nice having her close to him, feeling the warmth of her body so close to his.

He fumbled the key out of his pocket, opened the door. She helped him into the darkness, found the light switch, guided him across the living room and into the bedroom, where she lowered his gently to the bed. She sat down beside him, put a hand to his forehead.

"Feeling better?"

"Much," he said. Her hand was gentle, soothing and cool against his forehead, and on impulse, he put his hand over hers. In the dim light she looked very nice. She was wearing a tightfitting blouse, and the view from where he was was fantastic. Even with the throbbing pain in his skull, the situation was romantically intriguing.

Carla laughed. "You must be feeling better," she said. "If you keep looking at me like that, I may have to fight for my honor. By the way—" she brought something out of her pocket—"they dropped your wallet. Do you want me to notify the police?"

He thought a minute. "No," he decided. "I couldn't identify them."

"You could identify the girl," Carla suggested.

"I don't know for sure she was with them."

Carla shrugged. "Well, it's your business. I think you're making a mistake, though."

"I've made mistakes before," Gil said.

"Yes," she said evenly, "you have."

Gil didn't go into that. He felt sorry for Laura, the girl at the bar. Besides, it was his own fault, marching into an unfamiliar bar looking for a pickup; it was asking for trouble in a loud, clear voice.

"How did you happen to be around when I needed you?"

"I was worried about you. When you left the FLIGHT DECK you looked concerned, more than I think I've seen you look. And—and I knew you were in for some more fancy frustrating tonight. I was afraid you'd do something rash. I telephoned you, but there was no answer. I was on my way over to your place to see if you were all right, when I saw you fighting in the street. I must have scared your friends away." She hesitated. "Gil, it's none of my business, but are you going to marry Brenda Hamilton or aren't you?"

"Yes," Gil said.

It wasn't an easy thing to explain, so he didn't even try. Love is like that. It hits you and you're stuck with it.

"Fine," Carla said, without enthusiasm. "Then the two of you can go on Tourist Club excursions together."

"Maybe you and Murphy can come along with us and make it a double," Gil suggested, sarcastically.

"Maybe we could!" Carla said defiantly. She got up. "You'd better get some sleep, Gil. You'll need it to keep up with your society friend!"

She stamped from the room. Gil rose to his elbows and called, "Carla, wait!"

She didn't answer, so he rose from the bed and hurried through the darkened hallway into the living room. Carla had her hand on the doorknob. He went to her, placed a gentle hand on her arm.

"Carla, I'm sorry. I'm all mixed up. I don't know what's right and what's wrong anymore."

She sighed, and her breasts rose provocatively with the breath. "I guess I'm just living in the past, Gil. We used to be great friends."

He stepped in close to her, so that the tips of her sweatered breasts were touching him. He put his hands around her waists aware more than ever of the intense femaleness of her.

"Don't go, Carla," he said softly. "Stay with me. I need you."

Her dark eyes flashed. "Like you needed that girl at the bar?"

"Why did you come back then?" he asked her.

"Because I'm an idiot, that's why," she said. "Now look, Gil Baxter, if you want to be buddies, that's all right with me—but I'm not Brenda Hamilton and I'm not one of your pickups. I want you to remember that."

"I'll remember it," Gil said.

"Fine," she said. She turned the doorknob, kissed him on the forehead. "Now, be a good boy and go to bed."

"Alone?"

"Alone."

"I'm perfectly wide awake now. Let's take a ride ... in your M.G., if you like. It's been such a long time that we've talked. I promise to behave myself."

She hesitated visibly. "We used to have a lot of fun together, Gil," she said, softly. Then, with sudden enthusiasm, "Okay. I may even take you down to my place for a drink. How does that sound?"

"It sounds great," Gil said, meaning it. "Are you still living at the beach?"

She nodded. "With Maxine Benesch. You remember her."

Gil remembered her. Maxine was a chunky little brunette he never particularly liked.

"We've got a two bedroom place there," Carla said. "You can even sleep there tonight, if you want." She grinned at him. "Alone, that is. I'm holding out for marriage."

He grinned back at her. "I don't blame you," he said, straight-faced. "I'm doing the same thing!"

They went out to the M.G. and got in. Carla was driving, and there wasn't much opportunity for conversation. She headed the car onto the freeway and headed south, toward the beach cities. The wind whipped briskly around him, chasing the alcohol from his mind. It was nice being with Carla again, being in the same car, both of them heading in the same direction—geographically at least, if not emotionally.

But it couldn't be a late session. There was a lot to do tomorrow. He had to see Brenda. And Charlie Parker, perhaps. He might even arrange to have himself invited along on one of those excursions the Tourist Club was having in a few days. He couldn't shake the nagging feeling that there was some danger involved; the feeling was irrational, with not the remotest logic to help support it, but it was real nonetheless.

He forced the thoughts from his mind. Tomorrow was soon enough to take on Brenda and the entire Tourist Club single-handed. Tonight, there was Carla.

He glanced over at her as she wheeled the M.G. expertly along the concrete roadway, at the smooth, clean profile of her face, the feminine curves of her body. Murphy was a nice guy, and a lucky guy. Murphy deserved Carla. Tonight would be a platonic session, a matter of old friends getting together.

Except he still felt the age-old male stirring deep within him, and despite himself his eyes traced the female loveliness of Carla's legs so close to his own—and he was no longer certain that the night would pass without the fires of love being quenched in their own, natural ways.

CHAPTER FOUR

The trip to Redondo Beach was made in silence, the wind and the roar of the M.G. wiping out any attempts at conversation. Carla pulled off the freeway and onto a dark road that resembled a concrete roller coaster. At the peak of one hill, they could see the ocean, with a full moon hovering at the horizon, a brightly lighted fishing boat in the dark water seemingly suspended in mid-air.

They went down the hill and turned into an alleyway with houses crowded on either side. Carla parked on one side of the alley, next to a garage, cut the lights and the motor. A salt breeze brought them sounds of the nearby ocean.

"Come on," she said. "Maxine is probably still up. I can hear the radio playing."

She led him to a side door on the ground floor, opened it and went in. She turned to close the door and then stood close to him in the darkness, hesitating. Impulsively, her arms went around him, along his back, pulling him to her, and her lips found his and kissed him hungrily. She broke away.

"Well, a girl can change her mind, can't she? Besides, if one old friend can't kiss another old friend, then what are old friends for, anyway. Go on into the living room. I want to change my clothes and get us a couple of drinks."

She ducked into a hallway door and closed it. Gil walked straight ahead and around a bend and found himself blinking into the light of a living room, where two very startled people sat up and stared at him. Maxine and a male friend were sitting, more or less, on the couch. Maxine's blouse was unbuttoned and her skirt was up over her knees. Her boyfriend looked more annoyed than embarrassed.

"Now what the hell ..." the boyfriend said.

"Sorry," Gil stammered, turning to go, "I didn't know ..."

"You may as well stay," Maxine said with a resigned sigh. "I remember you. You're Gil Baxter, the pilot. I suppose Carla brought you home with her."

"Yes, she did," Gil admitted.

"This is my fiance, Scottie," Maxine said. "Scottie, this is Gil Baxter, a friend of Carla's."

Scottie grunted, but it was obvious he wasn't pleased to meet Gil. Gil couldn't blame the man, under the circumstances.

"Scottie and I are going to get married," Maxine volunteered. "We're saving up for it."

"That's nice," Gil said.

He plopped into an overstuffed chair, still feeling uncomfortable from having interrupted the two lovers. He was grateful that Carla came in, carrying a tray of glasses, mix, and icecubes.

"You should have phoned that you were coming," Maxine said, glaring at Carla.

"It was a spur of the moment thing," Carla said, and promptly dismissed the thought. "Who's for booze?"

She had changed to clinging blue housecoat, and from the jiggle it was obvious that this was the only garment she was wearing. Carefully, she poured a dollop of bourbon in each glass, plopped in a couple of ice cubes and filled the glass with mix.

"Nothing for us, thanks," Maxine said. "It's about time we got some rest." She yawned, got up, and pulled Scottie from the room.

Gil stared after them. Carla handed him a glass.

"Does he pay part of the rent?" Gil wanted to know.

Carla laughed softly. "Scottie is an unemployed truckdriver," she said. She went to the floor lamp and turned the switch until only one bulb glowed, sending a soft light around the room. "Maxine thinks she's in love with him."

"But she isn't?"

Carla shrugged. "It doesn't really matter. The important thing is, she's convinced she is, and she thinks that Scottie is going to marry her. She doesn't know he already has a wife and three kids in Kansas City."

Gil stared at her unbelievingly. "You haven't told her?"

Carla sat down on the couch. "Why should I? She's happy now. She'll find out sooner or later, I know, but the later it is the longer she'll be happy."

"But she might get pregnant ..."

"She's already pregnant," Carla said. And then annoyed, "Gil Baxter, are you coming over here and sit with me or aren't you?"

"That's the best offer I've had all day," Gil said, grinning.

He got up and carried his glass across the room, took a sip of the drink and then placed it on the coffee table. Carla's hair was disarrayed so that it made a feminine frame for her pretty face. Even in the dim lighting, her eyes glowed, her lips glistened with a moist sensuousness.

The radio was playing soft, romantic melodies, but they could still hear above it the sounds coming from the bedroom—the squeak of springs, the rustle of sheets, the sighs, the moans.

Carla moved toward him on the couch, the movement causing her robe to part and fall on either side of her bare legs. She put her head on his shoulder and her slim fingers worked at his collar and then rubbed his neck.

He reached for her, his heart beating wildly, his hands on her waist, feeling the warmth of her through the thin robe. His lips brushed hotly along her neck, up around her ear, and then quickly across to her half-parted lips which waited for him, expectantly, impatiently.

Their mouths blended in a long hard kiss. His tongue explored the inner surfaces of her lips in little darting movements. His hands moved across her back, pulling her closer to him, until he could feel her breasts jutting proudly against him, rising and falling with the increased frequency of her breathing.

The robe had fallen completely open, and in the dim light her flesh was smooth. He moved his hands across her.

"Not here," she whispered suddenly.

She rose, evading his reaching hands, and walked across the room. She paused at the door—to the outside—and smiled.

"You're going to have to work for this one, mister," she said. "Come on, if you dare!"

Gil got up, realizing what she had in mind. He recalled how they'd gone to a remote beach area of Connecticut one weekend during a summer together. It had been great fun—even the nude swims at midnight in the icy waters, mainly because of what had happened afterward. His pulse quickened at the thought.

Carla had a blanket in her hand. She smiled enticingly at him, opened the door and ran out into the night.

Gil followed her. It was cool and damp, with mist shrouding the air. He could hear the sound of her feet ahead of him.

"Come on, Gil," she said softly.

He shivered and then started after her, smiling grimly. It was a crazy, impulsive thing she was doing. But she did have the blanket, and besides it had been such a long time since he'd done a crazy impulsive thing.

He crossed the alleyway, made his way along a walk between rows of houses, and suddenly his feet touched sand. He could feel the ocean breeze more strongly, almost taste the salt of it, and its muted rumbling grew louder in his ears. He was getting closer to Carla; he could see her blue housecoated form ahead of him, hear the crunching of sand beneath her naked feet.

Suddenly, she was before him. She'd tossed the blanket on the ground and was standing a few yards from the water's edge. With a quick movement she stripped the house coat from her.

"Come on, catch me!" she yelled at him, and ran naked into the water.

Gil quickly took off his clothes and followed her into the surf. The night air was cold against his bare skin but the water was colder, and he winced as the first waves hit him. Then he plunged into the roaring water, which closed over him, blocking out all sight and sound.

A body came crashing into him, knocking the air from his lungs. He grabbed the body and surfaced, spluttering. Carla was laughing, holding on to him, as he held on to her and tried to cough the water out of his throat. Her body was slippery, and when he tried to pull her close to him, she evaded his grasp and ran up onto shore.

He went after her, up onto the sand. She was lying on her back on the blanket, holding its edges open.

"Come on, Gil," she said impatiently. "It's cold out there."

Already, Gil was shivering as the air contacted his wet body. He dropped down beside Carla, who closed the blanket around him. Her body was still wet, but it was warm and very nice. They snuggled together, while the fog swirled around them. They held each other very close, and the soft touch of her body against his gave Gil a comforting feeling that was much more than sexual. He felt very warm and secure being with Carla like this. It was very pleasant being with her. Brenda would probably not even consider going for a moonlight swim, and certainly not in the nude.

He frowned and realized quite suddenly that he was a real heel. It wasn't fair to Brenda that he should be playing around like this. And even worse, it wasn't fair to Carla.

He shook the thoughts from his mind and tried not to think of anything except how warm and comfortable it was under the blanket with Carla's naked body against him, protecting him from the cold fog and the waves reaching foaming fingers along the shore. He closed his eyes and submerged himself in the warm feeling. His body felt very relaxed, and all desire faded before contentment. It had been a long day, and a strenuous one, and he felt himself dozing.

The sounds of the wind and the waves seemed very far away. Gil was conscious only of the small wonderful world inside the blanket, and even that was fading quickly before the insistence of sleep.

The last thing he remembered was the gentle pressure of Carla's lips against his. He never even heard her say softly, longingly, almost reverently, "I love you, you stupid lug!"

CHAPTER FIVE

Gil fought his eyes open against the daylight, panic racing through him. He recalled that he had fallen asleep stark naked with Carla on the beach, and he could picture himself lying on the sand surrounded by curious, amused people.

His eyes snapped open, and his vision took in a bedroom ceiling with a pink-shaded overhead light, and he became aware of the bed he was in. He remembered then the sleepy return to the apartment, his collapsing on the bed, and Carla tucking him in. In seconds, he'd fallen into a deep, undreaming sleep.

He heard soft whispers from the next room, where Maxine and Scottie slept. Maxine was sighing contentedly.

"Just think, in only two more months, we'll have enough money, and we can get married. It'll be swell having our own little place, and you'll be in business for yourself and ..."

"Yeah," Scottie said, "I'm really looking forward to it, baby." He whispered something to her.

Maxine giggled. "Oh, Scottie, not now."

"Why?"

"Well ... because somebody might hear us, that's why."

"You mean the flyboy? He's probably still sacked out. He and your girlfriend were out late, probably went down to the beach." He chuckled. "Did you ever hear that joke about sand in the ..."

"Scottie, not so loud," Maxine said, shushing him.

"Well, if you don't want to talk, then how about ..." He whispered something to her again.

She giggled once more. "All right, Scottie, anything you say. I love you, Scottie."

"I love you too, baby," Scottie said. "Attagirl. Attagirl. Attagirl."

Gil forced his attention away from what was going on in the other bedroom. He wondered where Carla had gone off to. He also wondered where Brenda was right now, and if she'd called him at his apartment; he hoped she had called, and that she wondered where he was, for a change, though this didn't seem too likely. She'd be too busy making plans for the travel club outing. Which reminded Gil that he'd have to have a little chat with Charlie Clark, and the sooner the better.

Footsteps sounded on the walk outside, and the door banged open and shut.

"Hi ho, you lovebirds!" It was Carla, who moved into the kitchen and made noises about the stove and refrigerator. "I've bought doughnuts, bacon, and eggs to restore the sexual vitality of an eunuch."

Gil noticed, with embarrassment, that not only did he need no restorative methods, but that sometime during the night his natural functions had caused a release of the tension that had built up by the closeness of Jan, the girl at the bar, and Carla. It was inevitable that release would have to come, and Gil reflected that his body was wiser in certain respects than his mind.

Carla came bustling into the room. "Aren't you awake yet?"

"Not quite. But if you keep on shouting about food, you may have some effect."

"Are you sure it's food you want?" she said, grinning at him. "Which reminds me. You know, for one wild moment last night, I thought you were going to rape me."

"Uh-uh," Gil told her. "You know the old saying: never rape a buddy."

Carla was wearing tight short-shorts and a halter that barely contained her lush feminine curves, and she had zoris on her feet. She was very lovely, very female, very desirable.

"I'd better get some coffee going," she said, "before you change your mind and we never have breakfast." She paused at the door. "I put up some fresh towels in the bathroom, in case you'd like to shower. By the time you're through, breakfast should be ready."

Gil got up and threw a blanket over his shoulders to cover his nakedness. He went into the corridor, ignoring Carla's long whistle of appreciation, and went into the bathroom. As promised, there was a fresh linen awaiting him, and also a complete set of shaving equipment on the sink. Carla was a very thoughtful girl; she'd make a wonderful wife for some lucky guy.

The last thought brought a frown to his face, but he dismissed the depression he suddenly felt, and turned toward making himself presentable. It was an almost perfect way to start a vacation—a good sleep in a warm bed, an unhurried shave, a shower; all it lacked was one thing.

He stood under the shower with the water warm for a long time, until Carla banged on the door and wanted to know if he was going to spend his entire leave in there, and then he turned the faucet to cold and shivered with invigorated delight as the icy needles raked his body. He toweled his skin dry, wrapped himself in the blanket again, and retreated back to the bedroom.

Carla had washed and ironed his shirt, and his underwear and socks were still warm from the dryer. It was a pleasant surprise, and it made him feel very domestic and contented. He dressed quickly, then went into the kitchen to join the others.

They were at the table. Maxine and Scottie had already started, but Carla was just having a coffee, waiting for him.

"Sorry, I'm late," he apologized.

"It's your vacation," Carla pointed out. "You can laugh at schedules and appointments."

She brought him a hot platter of bacon, eggs and toast, with a large glass of orange juice on the side, and got one for herself. They ate, talking little. Gil wanted to say things to her, like how much he appreciated her having rescued him, not merely from the thugs the night before, but from the depression he'd found himself in because of Brenda. She was going way out of her way to understand, to make him feel very grateful.

But he didn't want to say anything in front of Maxine and Scottie, who were busy eating and grinning at each other.

"We'd better get going," Maxine said, when they were finished.

"Yeah," Scottie agreed.

They went to gather some belongings and then went out, not saying goodbye. There was the sound of a car starting, and then silence filled the rooms.

"They're going out to Long Beach amusement pier," Carla explained.

"I hope they don't get too emotional and fall out of the ferris wheel," Gil said with a grin.

Carla grinned knowingly back at him. "And what are your plans for today, young man?"

Gil sighed, remembering.

"Why not stay here," she suggested. "Just relax, make yourself comfortable. There's TV, books, a beach on the doorsteps, and if you want it, feminine companionship."

"You're tempting me," Gil told her honestly, "but I can't do it. My mind is full of ants; I couldn't sit still. I've got to find out once and for all what is going on with Brenda and that crowd of hers."

"Maybe it's just a travel club."

Gil shook his head. "Brenda's not the type to join an ordinary travel club. No, there's more to it than that, much more, but I don't know what. And frankly, Carla, it's got me worried. I'm afraid Brenda may be letting herself in for more than she suspects."

Carla slowly sipped at her coffee. Finally, she said, "Are you really in love with her, Gil?"

He hesitated, wondering if he should be honest with her and tell her that he wasn't really sure any more. Perhaps it was only a sense of obligation he felt, since it was his child Brenda was carrying.

Carla sensed his hesitation and said, "Never mind, Gil. One thing is certain: you've got to investigate this thing yourself and find out what's going on. How do you propose to start?"

"With Charlie Clark," Gil decided. "He's a member of the Country Club, but they won't let him into the Tourist Club. He pretends not to care, but I think he's secretly miffed by it and is willing to tell all he knows. In fact, he even invited me out to the place for a drink."

Carla got up, took the phone in her hands and brought it across the room to him. "Now's a good time to start," she suggested.

Gil nodded agreement and dialed the number of the Country Club. He asked for Charlie Clark, and a few minutes later the man's voice came on.

"This is Gil Baxter," Gil said into the phone. "I thought I'd take you up on that drink you offered me, if you're free this afternoon."

"Fine," Charlie Clark said enthusiastically. "I'd like that. About two o'clock be all right with you?"

"Yes, it would."

"Then two o'clock it is. Don't forget to mention my name, or you'll get the bum's rush. The guard takes his job more seriously than it deserves."

Gil hung up, and he felt a warm glow of satisfaction at having taken the first step toward finding out what was going on.

"Let me take a shower," Carla said, "and then I'll drive you back to your place." She stood up, "join me?"

He grinned at her, and automatically his eyes wandered over her body, mentally caressing the soft, yet firm, woman's flesh straining against the halter and spilling over at the top, and the tight shorts that clung to her hips and rounded behind. With an effort, he shook the thoughts from his mind.

"Uh ... I think I'll just sit here and read," he told her, picking up a magazine and sitting in a comfortable-looking chair facing the TV set.

"Okay," Carla said, "but in that case, I won't even let you look. I'm going to leave the bathroom door open so it'll be cooler, and I don't want you turning around to peek at me. Promise?"

"Promise," he said.

He turned his attention to the magazine, while Carla went into the bathroom. Some movement at the top of his vision caught his attention, and Gil looked up. He almost laughed in surprise and amusement. The bathroom, with its door open, was reflected in the glass of the silent TV screen. He felt a momentary pang of conscience and was tempted to mention the reflection to Carla. Then he decided against it. It would serve no purpose to tell her, and he could busy himself with the magazine and never look up at the screen at all.

He forced his eyes to the magazine, wondering what she was doing. He looked up.

Standing in the bathroom, Carla looked toward him. Then as though satisfied that he was not watching, she reached in back of her and unsnapped her halter, letting her breasts fall free. Then she unbuttoned and unzipped her shorts and worked them down over her hips, using a wiggling motion that would have been suggestive had it not been innocent. The brief, thin panties followed the course of the shorts.

Gil stared, unable to take his eyes off her reflection in the TV screen. He had found Carla beautiful and enticing before, but now, watching the surreptitious show of her magnificently rounded and curved body, he found her more appealing and sexier than ever.

She bent to take her shower cap from the cupboard, and then she put on the cap, tucking her flaming hair under the rim of it. Then she was through the shower curtains and out of his sight.

Her disappearance was like a breath of cold to his hot body. He felt himself annoyed to be reacting like a schoolboy peeping at a young girl undressing, and he forced his attention to the magazine. But the words refused to focus, and he found himself listening to the hum of the shower pelting her naked body, the gurgle of the water as it ran down the drain, found himself actually envying the water caressing that magnificent female body with liquid fingers.

The water stopped, and Gil's head automatically swiveled upward to the TV screen.

Carla's hand came out and took a towel. Then the curtain opened and she stepped out, still dripping, like some lovely goddess just arisen from the sea. She began rubbing her body briskly with the towel, starting at the shoulders and neck and moving along the well-formed breasts. Once again, he couldn't tear his eyes from the sight, and he felt his mouth go dry and his heart start to beat rapidly as he watched the towel make its leisurely way down over the hips, across the dimpled stomach, and along the smooth, silky legs.

Now dry, Carla stretched languorously, standing on tiptoe, her breasts rising taut with the movement. Then she sprayed herself with cologne and dusted her entire body with powder. Gil almost breathed an audible sigh of relief when she slipped on her housecoat and came into the room behind him.

He hastily directed his attention to the magazine, pretending not to notice her. He was glad it was over. The sight of her had been inspiring—and very frustrating. She bent down over him, and he could smell the soft female odor of her, blended with cologne and powder. His heart pounded at the knowledge that there was nothing on under the housecoat and that the slightest turn of his head would give him a close-up view of her, so close to him, so lovely and desirable, so much his for the asking.

It would be lovely to make love to her, and his soul ached with his want, his fast-growing need. Silently, he cursed his dedication to Brenda and his child that was in her, and he wished that somehow he could rationalize making love to this other woman who stood now beside him. But there was just no rationalization. It would simply not be fair, not even to Carla—and perhaps especially to her.

"Did you enjoy the magazine, Gil?" she asked.

She ran her slender fingers along the base of his neck, making the hairs there stand on end.

Gil hadn't noticed what he'd been looking at, but at her words his eyes focused, and he discovered that he had in his hands a woman's magazine opened at an article on what to do and not to do on "those" days of the month. Hastily, he closed the magazine, and looked up at her. She was grinning at him, and he wondered if she knew he'd been watching her. He wouldn't put it past her to do something like that on purpose, not maliciously but hoping to tease and taunt him.

"Made any plans?" she asked him seriously.

"I thought I'd see what Charlie Clark had to say first. I'll just play it by ear until I have something more concrete to work on."

She leaned over him to give a platonic peck on his cheek. Then she straightened, hesitating.

"Gil, is there any hope that you'll forget this investigation of yours? You said you thought it might be dangerous for Brenda. Well, it might also be dangerous for you, possibly even more so."

Gil shrugged. "It's a chance I'll have to take, Carla." He patted her hand. "Thanks for your concern. You'd better get dressed if I'm going to make that appointment."

Carla opened her mouth as though to say something, then decided to close it instead. Then she went into the bedroom to dress. A moment later she came out in halter and shorts and announced she was ready. They went out to the M.G.

Gil drove. They took the Coast Highway, and the conversation was slight as each seemed lost in his own thoughts. Occasionally, Gil glanced over at Carla, at her fine lovely features and flowing red hair, at the firm breasts straining at the halter, at the small golden hairs of her gently-curved legs gleaming in the sunlight.

They pulled to a stop in front of Gil's apartment. He opened the door and stepped out, and Carla slid across the seat to the wheel.

"Call me as soon as you know something, she said.

"I will," he promised. He paused. "Carla, you've been wonderful."

"Sure," she said, wryly, "I've been a buddy!" She shifted the M.G. into gear. "Get going now. And—and be careful."

With a roar, she sped away. Gil watched her disappear around a corner, and then he went to his apartment. It was almost one o'clock. He thought of what Carla had said about it being dangerous to investigate the Tourist Club activities. He'd had that same feeling himself. Something was going on with that group that wasn't right. They were too secretive, almost fanatically so, and they wouldn't accept an intruder lightly.

Nevertheless, in another hour, Gil knew, he would start getting some answers to some very important questions!

CHAPTER SIX

From the outside, the Arroyo Country Club resembled a cemetery, and Gil wondered grimly if there might be something significant about the resemblance. It was quiet, peaceful, tucked away in a neat, remote corner away from the noisy, frantic traffic of the world. Large trees bordered acres of greenness punctuated by lawn sprinklers and an occasional tropical bush.

Gil drove the black Jaguar up the concrete road leading from the street, along the entranceway guarded by tall sentinel palm trees which regarded him impassively. A steel gate barred the road ahead, and at his approach a brawny uniformed guard stepped from the gatehouse, his face anything but impassive.

Gil drew up sharply and stuck his head out.

"Members only," the guard growled.

"And their guests," Gil reminded him. "Charlie Clark invited me. My name's Gil Baxter."

The guard's eyebrows rose a fraction of an inch. His bulldog face was unimpressed.

"Wait here," he said.

He turned on his heel and returned to the gatehouse, where he picked up a telephone from the wall. He talked confidentially into the phone, then cradled the instrument and came back out.

"You can go in," he said, but his tone wasn't any more polite.

"Thanks a lot," Gil said drily.

The guard ignored the sarcasm and touched a button that noiselessly opened the gate. Gil noticed the man glared as the

Jaguar went past. *"Now what's wrong with him?"* Gil wondered, and then shrugged it off. He was probably resentful of the rich enjoying themselves at the club while he had to sit by himself in the gate house. Everybody had problems.

Gil drove up the road toward the large white building gleaming in the California sun. A slim young man appeared, took his car and whipped it into a parking place among the Cadillacs and Lincolns. Then he walked up the flagstone walk toward the steps, where a man was standing, holding a drink in one hand and motioning to him with the other.

The man was about sixty years old, with grey hair, a thin, angular, wrinkled face and pale blue eyes peering from under massive eyebrows. His frail frame was encased in light blue trousers, a dark blue jacket, a white sportshirt open at the neck. For some reason, he reminded Gil of a retired English ambassador.

"Charlie Clark?" Gil said.

"Right," Charlie Clark said in a thin voice, extending his hand, "and you're Gil Baxter, of course. Let's go inside and get ourselves a drink. At my age, that's about all the club is good for, the drinks. They make wonderful Tom Collinses. Great on a warm afternoon."

Charlie led the way across the shaded porch and through the door into the dark coolness of the bar. The room was air conditioned, and it was like going into a refrigerator from the heat of the outside. Charlie made his way through the dimness to an isolated table in a corner by a huge unlit stone fireplace and signaled for a waiter.

"Another Collins for me, George," he said, "And something for Mr. Baxter."

"I'll have a Collins, too," Gil said.

The waiter went to get the drinks.

"Nice little place you have here," Gil said.

Charlie laughed, good-naturedly. "It is a cozy little nook, isn't it. We've got a hundred acres all to ourselves. There's something for everybody here—horseback riding, tennis courts, a swimming pool, a bar ..."

"Even a tourist club," Gil said.

Charlie nodded grimly. "Even a tourist club." He stared thoughtfully at Gil for a moment. "Do you know anything at all about the tourist club, Gil?"

"Not as much as I'd like to. Except it must be a very special type of club to attract Brenda, and to hold her. I actually think she'd stand me up on our honeymoon if it conflicted with one of their tours!"

"Ah, here are our drinks," Charlie said. "Yes, in a way I suppose you're right, but if the Dodgers could keep up the kind of playing that they were then, I'm sure they can win the pennant."

The waiter brought two frosted glasses filled with ice and liquid.

"Thank you, George," Charlie said to the waiter, and to Gil, "Say what you will, I still think the Dodgers ..."

He continued talking baseball until the waiter had moved out of earshot, then he sipped appreciatively at his drink for a moment.

"Don't even mention the travel club in front of anyone here unless it comes up in conversation. In fact, don't ever mention anything in front of these fellows that you don't want the front office to know."

"You're making it sound very mysterious," Gil said.

"It is mysterious," Charlie said, "and intentionally so. Fifty years ago my father founded this club. There was money in the family then, and—well, that's another story. But, at any rate, the club represented wealth, prestige, position—and more importantly—dignity." He sighed. "Until the last few years."

"And now?" Gil prompted.

"The community still thinks of the club as the last strong-hold of solid wealth and dignity. Thank goodness, we've never been foolish enough to wash our dirty linen in public."

"You say the last few years. What happened?"

"About five years ago we began running into a little bad luck. Some of the younger members were restless felt that we were behind the times, living in the past. At their insistence—because we couldn't afford to lose them as members—we got a new manager, a man named Edmund Beaubelle. That was the worse mistake the club has ever made. Since that time, the club has become a haven for all kinds of strange people. The guards at the gate were his idea; sometimes I think they have more of a say in the club than some of us older members. Memberships have been sold to people who wouldn't even have been considered ten years ago."

"I see," Gil said slowly.

Charlie shook his head sadly. "Edmund and his obscene sis-ter Mari have just about got the club sewed up. They're not only members themselves, but they're on the board of directors and are leaders of the tourist club!"

"I can see this is a very personal thing with you, Charlie," Gil said. "I'm curious as to why you're telling me all this. I'm not a member, and it looks like I'm never going to even qualify."

"I like you, Gil," Charlie said sincerely. "I can see you're already caught up emotionally in this mess because of your love for Brenda, and I'd like to help you straighten her out and your lives as well. And yes, let's face it, I'd like to find out myself what's going on around here."

"You think I'll be able to, without being a member?"

"I think you're in a much better position to than I am. If I did it—and I've tried—I'd be merely snooping. They're very careful around me, they know I've got my nose all primed to sniff any hint of a scandal. Before, I might have tried to cover up anything I found, in memory of what was. But now—well, frankly, Gil, I'm worried. The travel club is more than just a travel club, I'm sure of that. It …" he hesitated, then rushed on, "it might even be dangerous to the members, to your Brenda, for instance."

Gil nodded somberly. "I was afraid it might. If they're so secretive, there must be a good reason they don't want anyone to find out what they're doing. Can you tell me anything more about it?"

"Not much, I'm afraid. They've got another trip coming up in a few days—to Mexico, I think, someplace in Baja California south of San Felipe. They're in a soundproof clubroom discussing it right now." He glanced at his watch. "In fact, they could come in here for a drink at any minute, and if you're going to be a spy for the good guys, we don't want them to see you. Perhaps we'd better adjourn our little meeting and get together someplace else at a later time."

"Okay," Gil said, standing. "Meanwhile, I'll do what investigating I can."

Charlie took a slip of paper from his inside breast pocket and wrote a name and address on it. He gave it to Gil.

"You may want to start there," Charlie said.

Gil nodded. The paper said, "Mari Beaubelle," and listed a Wilshire Boulevard address in the *"Miracle Mile"* area. He felt Charlie's hand on his arm.

"Some of them are coming in now. We'd better go out the back way."

Gil allowed himself to be led across the room. Charlie paused and nodded back at the bar.

"Do you see that striking blonde, the tall one a little bit older than the others? That's Mari Beaubelle."

Gil started, fascinated. Striking was indeed the word for Mari Beaubelle. She was tall, willowy, and her tight dress showed that she was endowed with plentiful curves. Charlie pulled at his arm, and Gil followed the man outside.

"But watch out for her brother," Charlie Clark said. "He's very happy with his job here, and he's the type who would do anything to keep it."

"I'll be careful, Charlie," Gil said, extending his hand, "and thanks very much. I'll certainly do whatever I can."

Charlie Clark's handshake was firm. "I hope for your sake, and for Brenda's sake before it's too late, and mine too, that you find out something."

Gil returned to the parking lot and took the black Jaguar down the hill again toward the gatehouse. He was thinking of Mari Beaubelle and of what a pleasure it would be to see her. He stopped before the steel gate and waited for it to open. Instead, the guard came out, showing his teeth in an unpleasant smile.

"Mr. Baxter," he said with exaggerated politeness. "The Executive Caommittee of the Arroyo Country Club has asked me to pass on a message to you. They say you are not welcome here, and hope you have the good sense to stay away."

"Really," Gil said. "Did they say why?"

The guard shrugged. "I only work here. They told me if you ever show your face around here, I shouldn't let you in."

Gil could feel the anger rising in him. "And you can tell the 'executive committee'," he said hotly, "to go to hell. I'm a guest of Charlie Clark, and I'll come up here any damned time I please!"

"You do," the guard said slowly, "and I'll toss you out on your ear!"

Gil appraised the guard. The man was large, chesty, muscular under the grey uniform, and his bulldog face was belligerent.

"Anytime you'd like to try it," Gil said, "let me know."

The guard's smile widened into a grimace. He slammed one large fist into an open palm, expectantly.

"How about right now?" he said.

Gil pulled the handbrake on the Jag, left the motor running. He stepped out of the car without opening the door. The guard had spread his feet to get a more solid footing and was standing, fists clenched at his side, grinning expectantly. Gil felt the blood boil in his veins. All during the frustration with Brenda, he'd wished he could have a rival he could fight—and now he had one in the person of this insolent guard who represented the club. It was a good feeling.

He was three feet away when the guard swung, suddenly without warning, putting everything he had into the blow. Gil ducked beneath the big fist, slashing with the edge of his hand at the big man's forearm. Then he stepped closer and slammed a right fist, with the knuckle extended, into the man's midriff, where it made a satisfying thump.

The guard doubled up, eyes closed in pain, and Gil raised his hand to slam it down at the base of the man's skull. Then he hesitated, and merely walked around to the gatehouse to press the button that would swing open the gate. He found it, pressed it, and the gate swung noiselessly aside.

"Harvey!" A feminine voice, sharp, insistent.

Gil whirled. The guard was on one knee, recovering. He had one hand inside his coat, as though reaching for a gun. But what took Gil's attention was the power-blue Thunderbird that had come up behind his Jaguar, or more specifically the blonde in the Thunderbird, looking very beautiful and very angry as she glanced from him to the guard. Gil recognized her as the one Charlie Clark had pointed out as Mari Beaubelle. Nodding briefly to her, which she did not acknowledge, he returned to the Jaguar, released the brake and drove through the open gate.

He glanced back to see Mari standing beside the guard, arguing with him, while he was gesticulating violently in the direction of the retreating Jaguar.

Mari was probably bawling him out for fighting with a guest, but why the use of the man's first name. Unless the rich did this as a matter of course with the hired help, or more likely, from the guard's attitude, he was a relative the Beaubelle's had given a job.

In any event, the guard would certainly be no friendlier toward him. From the looks of the man's hand going into his coat, he'd been armed and quite ready and willing to use his weapon. Mari had saved Gil's life—but it was probably that she wanted to avoid a scandal more than anything else. Charlie Clark had warned him to be careful, and it looked like there was good reason for it.

CHAPTER SEVEN

When Gil entered his apartment, the phone was ringing.

"Where have you been, darling?" It was Brenda, sounding very sweet and friendly. "I've been calling and calling. I was about to give up when you answered."

"Oh, I had a few errands to run. Things pile up when you're away as much as I am."

"I suppose so." She hesitated. "Gil, you were out at the Country Club today, weren't you?"

"Yes," Gil said.

There seemed to be little use in denying it. For a "spy" his movements were apparently well known.

"Gil, I told you I didn't want you spying on me," she said.

"I wasn't spying on you. I was just having a sociable drink with Charlie Clark."

"Oh, him."

"He seems like a nice guy."

"He's a busybody, a fuddy-duddy, an old man with an over-active imagination. He would just as soon have the Country Club stagnate and not have any excitement at all going on."

"Like the Travel Club," Gil volunteered.

"Yes, for one thing," she said. "What did he tell you?"

"We just talked," Gil said. "He was lonely and wanted an ear to bend, that's all."

"Is that really all, Gil?"

"Yes," he lied. "Why are you so worried about someone finding out anything about your precious travel club?"

She sighed. "Let's not go into that again, Gil. Please."

"Fine with me, Brenda," Gil said. "Let's got together tonight and see some bright lights, and I promise not to even mention anything controversial."

"All right, Gil," she said, and he could almost see her smile over the phone. "It's been a long time, it seems, since we've been together."

"Much too long. I hope it won't be long before we won't ever have to stay apart."

"I hope, so, too, darling," she said. "I'll see you later, then."

"About eight," Gil promised, and hung up.

He dialed Carla's number.

"Hello, Gil"?

"You're psychic," he said.

"Sure. Besides, I've been hanging around the phone for two hours waiting for you to call. I was afraid something had happened to you."

"Well, nothing has yet, but I do have a lead. I'm sure more than ever there's something fishy about the travel club. I was talking with Charlie Clark, and he seems to think it might even be dangerous."

"Is there anything I can do to help?"

He hesitated. "There might be, Carla, But I hate to get you involved in this."

"I don't mind," she said. "I'll help you in any way I can, Gil. That's what friends are for."

Gil didn't remind her that she'd be also doing this for Brenda. He said, "I was seen at the club by one of the directors, a woman named Mari Beaubelle. I understand she runs a modeling agency in the Miracle Mile, but it could be a front for something else."

"It would be better if you didn't show yourself just now," Carla agreed. "Let me check that for you. I don't have a flight out until nine tonight, so I'll have time."

"I'd appreciate it, Carla. But don't put yourself in a spot. Just pretend you're a model, or a would-be model, and see if the agency is on the up-and-up. And call me as soon as you get out of there."

"Will do." She paused. "Oh, Gil?"

"Yes?"

"When you mentioned that name Mari Beaubelle it sounded familiar. Now, I remember where I'd heard it. In fact, I'm surprised I could forget something like that. She flew on one of my flights about six months ago—a tall, good looking blonde with plenty of curves."

"That sounds like her. What happened."

"Oh, she and some young guy got on the plane pretty well fried—and within twenty minutes they were trying to have sex right there in the airplane seats. She had her dress up around her navel, and the guy wasn't too well-covered up either before we managed to calm them down. Some councilman and his wife were sitting across from them, and they raised a fuss and threatened to sue the airline. I got the job of prying the two lovers apart; they weren't too happy with me."

"Do you think she'll recognize you?"

"I doubt it. She was too far gone."

"Anyway, don't get involved."

"I won't. I'll go over there now and give you a call in a couple of hours."

They hung up, and for a moment Gil stared at the phone without seeing it, thinking about the perverse fates that had made him fall in love with Brenda instead of Carla. Of course, the fact that she was carrying his baby helped. And Carla undoubtedly knew that by helping him solve the mystery of the travel club, she'd be helping him and Brenda get together—unless she thought the solution might force them apart. He shook his head wearily, realizing the futility of trying to analyze the complex motivations of a woman.

He got himself a cold beer from the refrigerator, took off his shoes, and stretched out on the couch with an Eric Thomas novel. He found himself fidgeting, however, and his attention strayed. He glanced constantly at his watch, where the hands seemed to move with incredible slowness, and he wondered how Carla was doing. She was probably in the big building in the Miracle Mile right now, talking to Mari Beaubelle.

Angry with himself, Gil threw down the book. He shouldn't have asked Carla to do this for him. It wasn't fair to her, and it might even be dangerous. At first, he'd thought it would be a simple matter of her going in and looking around and that would be it. But the members, and especially the directors, he supposed, would be not only secretive but suspicious, and suppose Mari remembered Carla from the airline and perhaps even sensed the link between the stewardess and Gil Baxter. If they though the operation was in jeopardy, who knows what they might do.

He considered driving out to the Beaubelle office, then thought better of it. He might miss Carla there, and he would certainly miss her promised telephone call. He picked up the novel again and tried to get interested in the intricate plot.

At five o'clock the phone rang.

"Gil?"

"Carla," he said, breathing a sight of relief, "thank heaven you're safe."

He could almost hear her grin of pleasure over the phone. "For a while I didn't think you cared," she said. "But why shouldn't I be safe?"

"No reason, I guess. I was just sitting here imagining all sorts of evil things happening to you. How'd it go?"

"All right," she said. "We'd better not talk too much, because I'm still in the Beaubelle office—in a separate room, but you never know who might be listening. Everything seems on the up and up, but I'm going to check it out further. Mari says there's a job coming up in a few days, but I've got a special interview in another fifteen minutes with her brother Edmund, who's a doctor in the same building here."

For some reason, Gil felt suddenly cold. "A special interview?"

"I should learn more about it then," she suggested.

"Carla, don't go," Gil said, on impulse.

"What?"

"No, I'm sorry I got you mixed up in this. Just leave right now and forget about it."

"Don't be silly," she said. "This could be our big chance to find out what's going on. Look, I'd better go. I'll call you back later."

Before he could protest, she'd hung up. He thought of calling her back, but that would involve all sorts of complications. For one thing, he didn't know, what name she was using there. Besides, she was right—in a special interview she might learn some valuable things; it was an opportunity that might not come again.

He was beginning to feel very foolish for having suggested she not go through with it. Of course, everything would be all right. There was really no reason for it not to. Even if the Beaubelles discovered what Carla was up to, they'd only tell her to leave, and the situation would be no worse than it had been before.

He felt a little better for the rationalization and settled back to do some more reading until she called him. An hour passed, and the phone was silent. Were "special" interviews that long?

And what was so special about them? And didn't she know he was starting to go out of his mind again with concern for her? The thought occurred to Gil that Carla might indeed know of his concern and wanted him to worry, perhaps not so much for revenge but out of a female satisfaction in knowing a man cared for her. He dismissed that thought, however. Carla was not the type. Brenda might, but not Carla. She'd call him as soon as she could.

Meanwhile, he took a shower and a shave, and when he was through it was close to seven o'clock. He picked up the phone and dialed a number. Miles away, in Redondo Beach, Carla's home phone began ringing. Gil let it ring a dozen times, and finally a panting, irritated female voice answered.

"Carla?" Gil said anxiously.

"This is Maxine," the girl said. "Carla's not here. Is that you, Gil?"

"Yes, Maxine. Carla was supposed to call me. Have you heard from her?"

"No, I haven't. Look, Gil, I'm in the middle of something ..."

"Come on, Maxine!" a male voice said near the phone on the other side.

"I'll give her you message, Gil," Maxine said, and hung up.

Gil stared at the phone as though refusing to believe the connection had been broken. He could imagine what Maxine had been in the middle of. He didn't really blame her for being irritated at the interruption. He could understand it himself. He replaced the receiver in the its cradle and sat down in the chair beside it, wishing it to ring.

In ten minutes it didn't ring, and he began to fidget. He glanced at his watch. He'd have to start getting ready for the date with Brenda. He shouldn't have made the date, but it had been so long since he and Brenda had been together. Yet the phone call from Carla was now becoming more important, and be considered calling Brenda and telling her he'd be late or even that he couldn't make it.

No, that was foolish. This could be a real beginning for him and Brenda, and he mustn't louse it up. Besides, Carla was supposed to report to the Flight Office of Trans-U.S. at nine o'clock. She couldn't miss that appointment. He waited twenty more minutes, until seven-thirty, but the phone didn't ring.

He dressed slowly, knowing he would be late anyway, but by eight o'clock he was ready and the phone still had not rung. He waited fifteen minutes more, then sighed and opened his front door to leave.

The phone rang.

With a glad cry, Gil strode to the phone, yanked it to his ear. "Carla?" he said.

There was an icy silence. "This is Brenda, Gil," the girl said. "I'm sorry to disappoint you, but our dates was for eight o'clock, and I'm starving. However, if you have something better to do ..."

"No, no, of course not," Gil stammered, glad she could not see his embarrassment. It reminded him of the time he had been with Jan under very intimate circumstances and called her Carla, and the uncomfortable faux pas feeling was with him again. "I'm sorry I'm late. My stewardess was supposed to call me with some information. I thought you were her."

"Well, I'm not," Brenda pointed out. "Are you coming over or not?"

"I was just leaving when you called," Gil told her. "I'll be right there."

The phone clicked dead. Gil stared at the phone again, knowing there was no use in waiting any longer. Carla probably had a long interview. If the club was so secretive, and the modeling operation was a part of it in some way, the'd want to very thorough. And perhaps she didn't have time to call him before rushing to the Flight Office for work. She might even have been trying to get him while he was talking to Brenda.

He left the apartment and paused briefly outside the door as though expecting the phone to ring. Then he went out to the Jaguar, got in and drove out onto the street. The night was clear and comfortably cool, and the stars were hard diamonds on black velvet. Brenda lived in a big house in Beverly Hills, and to get there from his Hollywood apartment Gil didn't have to drive down to Wilshire Boulevard and through the Miracle Mile district. But he did. And he parked briefly across the street from the large white brick building that housed the offices of the Beaubelle Modeling Agency; he turned out the lights of the car but left the motor running and stared up the side of the building, at the random pattern of the lighted windows, as the evening traffic drifted noisily past him.

On impulse, he cut the motor, got out of the Jag and jay-walked across the street and entered the building. The lobby was deserted. A desolate cigar stand stood silently in one corner next to a pair of empty telephone booths. A self-service elevator was at the opposite end of the lobby.

A wall directory told Gil that "Beaubelle, Mari. Modeling Agency" was in room 703. He got in the elevator and punched the seven button. The doors came together and the elevator whirred into motion. During the brief upward ride, Gil wondered what he would do if he ran into Carla or one of the Beaubelles. Just play it would be the best thing, perhaps even pretend that he was looking for a job himself.

Then the doors snapped open he stepped out into a silent, empty corridor. He walked down the hall, looking for room 703, trying to soften the hard click his feet made in the silence. All the doors were solid, with no glass, but no lights showed under any of the doors. He stopped before 703, which bore the same legend as on the wall directory. Room 705 had a sign which said, "Edmund Beaubelle, M.D." Gil wondered if the two offices were connected—by doors and perhaps by purpose as well. He stood quietly in the hall and listened. No sounds came from either of the two offices, so after a few minutes Gil retreated down the corridor to the elevator and descended to the street.

In the Jaguar he glanced at his watch. Eight-thirty five. Carla was probably on her way to the Flight Office to report in. He could give her a call there. Meanwhile, there was Brenda to consider.

When he arrived, she opened the door herself. She had her hair piled up in a golden monument on her head, and she was wearing a tight gold dress that fit her curves very tightly. She was beautiful, but her eyes flashed angrily.

"Sorry, I'm late," Gil apologized. "It couldn't be helped. Business."

She smiled sweetly. "Of course, Gil. Shall we go?"

They went. They drove in silence to Frascati's on the Sunset Strip. It was crowded and sounds of conversation lingered in the air and mingled with the smooth sounds of a piano and bass drifting from one corner. They sat down and ordered cocktails and Gil looked at his watch.

Brenda frowned. "I hope I'm not keeping you from something important," she said.

Gil forced a laugh. "I'm sorry. Excuse me, I've got to make a telephone call."

It was nine-twenty, and he wasn't in the mood to concoct excuses to Brenda for his abrupt behavior. He had to be certain Carla was safe, and he also had to find out what she had learned from interview. He made his way to the phone and dialed the number of Trans-U.S. He asked for the Flight Office, and a familiar voice answered.

"Hello, Jan, this is Captain Gil Baxter."

"Yes, Captain Baxter," Jan Sherwood said. There was a faint amusement in her voice, which annoyed Gil. "What can I do for you, if anything?"

"I wanted to get in touch with a stewardess," Gil told her, "named Carla O'Brien. She was supposed to report in at nine o'clock."

"Carla, eh?" Jan said thoughtfully. "It seems to me I've heard that name before. No, she hasn't reported in. Another girl took her place. Do you know where she is, Captain?"

Gil frowned worriedly. "No, I'm afraid not. I wish I did, thought.

"She must certainly be a popular girl," Jan said. "Someone else called about her early this evening."

Gil's heart turned cold. "Who?"

"He didn't say. A man with a slight French accent. He called about six-thirty, wanted to know if she was working for us, and if she was married. I got the impression she was applying for another job and this was her potential employer checking up on her. No wonder she didn't show up."

Gil made a sudden decision. "Jan, will you do me a favor?"

"Sure," Jan said, "for old time's sake."

Gil ignored the sarcasm. "If someone calls up to check on me, will you tell them I've been laid off for an indefinite length of time. It's very important."

Apparently, she was impressed by the seriousness of his tone. "All right, Captain, and I don't even ask you why? How's that for self control?"

"Thanks, Jan. And about last night … I am sorry. Really."

"Forget it. I can compete in the field of sex, but I always lose against true love. The story of my life. If your girl friend comes in, where shall I have her call you?"

"At Frascati's, the one on the Strip. Or at home."

"Will do."

Gil hung up. He found himself dreading the return to Brenda. He thought of what Jan had said, and he wondered if he were really in love with Carla as she'd intimated.

And he wondered where Carla was right now. She wasn't at home, she wasn't at the airline where she hould have been, and she wasn't at the office of the Beaubelle's. It hurt to think that wherever she was it was his fault that she was there. He clenched his fists in quiet seething anger as he thought about it. Carla would have to be all right. She'd have to. The thought of anything happening to her was too much to bear. He'd find her if he had to take on the Beaubelle's and every one of the members of their travel club single-handed.

And he knew that it was true what Jan had said. It had been true for some time, and his affection and sense of obligation to Brenda had blinded him to it—he was in love with Carla O'Brien!

CHAPTER EIGHT

The date with Brenda should have been a dream. She was lovely, they were unofficially engaged, the setting was romantic—and it was a nightmare.

No matter how he tried, Gil could not tear his thoughts away from Carla. He wondered a dozen times if he should go to the police, and decided a dozen times that he shouldn't. If Carla had met with any foul play, the police would only drive her more underground. Besides, she could take care of herself, and probably the only reason she hadn't contacted him was that it would be unwise to try.

Tomorrow, he would investigate the matter himself. The problem was getting through the evening. It wouldn't be easy, for Brenda demanded attention. Any other time, he would have been anxious to display all the attention she desired. But this night, not knowing what had happened to Carla, it was difficult.

They had cocktails and a dinner, and afterward Gil tried to drink enough to relax him. Instead, he smoked incessantly, and was constantly glancing at his watch.

Finally, around twelve-thirty, Brenda said, "What's on your mind, Gil?"

"Nothing," he lied. "Why?"

"Because you've been acting like there has been, that's why." She smiled at him and placed a hand on this. "Come on, tell me."

He looked at her and wondered if he should tell her that he'd decided he was in love with Carla and not with her. He wondered how she'd take the news. Would she be indignant? Hurt? Brave? Somehow, he could picture her being each of these. But then what? An abortion by some Mexican doctor, perhaps—a surgical removal of all the ties between Gil and Brenda. No more concern over the travel club?

He loved Carla, yet he wasn't at all certain he didn't love Brenda, too, in another, different but valid way. At the least, he liked her, he'd grown very fond of her, and if she were in some danger with the travel club he couldn't leave her now.

"As long as you asked," he said, adding parenthetically, "and you did ask, remember—I'm worried about this new trip of yours."

"Gil, really!" Brenda said.

"There are a lot of things you've never told me about your trips, Brenda. Look, I've got a right to know what's going on."

"And I've got a right to lead my own life!" she shot back at him, her eyes angry. "I can't take this constant prying of yours, Gil. You've got to have some faith, or there's no use our continuing our relationship. You weren't just having a sociable drink with Charlie Clark today. You were trying to find out information about the Travel Club."

"I was worried about you. In fact, I still am. I don't know what's going on, but I don't like it."

"Well, I do. I like it just fine, Gil Baxter, and not you or anybody else is going to tell me how to run my life!" She stood up. "Take me home!"

"Gladly," Gil said.

He paid the check and followed her out to the car. The drive to her place was silent and cold. Gil wanted to ask her about the baby, what she was planning on doing about it—but the words stuck in his throat. He tried to tell himself that lots of guys get lots of girls pregnant—it's one of the natural hazards of making love—without feeling such an intense obligation. Besides, Brenda, with her influence, could probably have the job taken care of locally. He was surprised at his matter-of-fact attitude toward the situation, and also ashamed that he actually felt some measure of relief to be off the hook.

Perhaps tomorrow his attitude would be different, but this night he felt emotionally dry with concern over what had happened to Carla, and all other things had become of secondary importance.

He pulled the Jaguar into the circular driveway in front of Brenda's house. He turned toward her, not knowing what to say.

"Brenda …"

"Goodnight, Gil," she said coldly, opened the door and stepped out.

He watched her slim form move up the steps and through the front door, which seemed to close with an ominous finality. Then, he accelerated the Jag down the hill to Sunset Boulevard and down Sunset to his own apartment.

He felt perfectly wide awake and cold sober. He poured a large snifter of brandy and sat on the bed and stared at the clock. One thirty. He picked up the phone and dialed Carla's number. After a dozen rings with no one answering, he hung up. If Carla had been there, she would have answered. Maxine and Scottie either weren't there, or they didn't want to bother.

Gil steadily poured the brandy into him and felt the warm glow of it permeate his insides. Then he went to bed, turned out the lights and tossed and turned restlessly until morning …

Morning came, and Gil found himself very tired. He was aware that he'd gotten only a few hours sleep during the night, but mucho of what he felt was weariness and the sense of helpless frustration in not being able to do anything for Carla.

He tried her home phone again, and Maxine answered.

"Gil, I'm worried," Maxine said, and her voice sounded it. "It's not like Carla to stay out like this. Maybe we should notify the police."

"Not yet," Gil said. "I want to check something this morning. I'll let you know if I find out anything."

He hadn't really expected Carla to be home. She would have called him if she could. That left only one thing for him to do.

First, he showered and shaved, and after a cup of hot black coffee he felt more human. He dressed, went out and had a solid breakfast, and ten o'clock he pushed his way through the door that said, "Room 703. Mari Beaubelle Modeling Agency."

It was a large room, heavily carpeted, with abstract painting bordering the walls, a massive oak desk crouched in one corner, a chair in front of the desk, a long leather couch against one wall. A grey filing cabinet was beside the couch close to one corner. The window looked out over Wilshire Boulevard traffic. As Gil had suspected, there was a closed door leading to room 705, Edmund Beaubelle's office.

Mari looked up from some paper work she was doing, and Gil thought her eyes flickered with interest as she glanced at him. Her blonde hair, loose the day before, was pulled tightly to her and fastened in back, and she was wearing horn-rimmed glasses; neither maneuver made her look less pretty, especially in the tight black dress she was wearing. There seemed to be a hungry quality to her lips.

"What can I do for you?" she said.

Gil closed the door behind him and walked toward her. "My name is Gil Baxter. I'm looking for a job."

She looked thoughtfully at him. "Haven't I seen you someplace before, Mr. Baxter?"

Gil was honest with her. "Yesterday, at the Country Club. I got in a fight with the guard at the gate."

"Oh, yes. Harvey is sometimes rather impetuous. He didn't like you."

"I didn't care much for him, either," Gil said.

"I could tell," she said, laughing. "You made pretty short work of him, and he's a big man, too." Her eyes flicked over his chest, and she took a breath. "You seem to be a pretty muscular fellow."

"Thanks. I picked up a little Judo and Karate in the Orient. That helps."

"I'm sure it would," she said. "Harvey said you were visiting one of our members—Charlie Clark."

"I needed a job, and I thought Charlie might know of something. He said you were running a model agency and maybe you could use me. So here I am."

"Have you ever done any modeling before?"

"No," he admitted. "I've been with airlines, but I was laid off a couple days ago. I've kept myself in pretty good physical condition, do some weight lifting, did some wrestling and boxing in college."

"Take off your shirt," she said.

Gil took off the jacket, placed it across the chair, started unbuttoning his shirt. Mari's eyes glittered at his movements, and she got up and moved toward him as he stripped the shirt from his body. An involutary gasp of delight tore from Mari's throat as she saw his nudity, and she raised her hands as thought wanting to run her hands across his chest.

Gil found himself doing some watching of his own. Mari's black dress was very tight and clinging, unspoiled by any rim of bra or panty. It was obvious she had a full, perfect figure under the dress, and probably nothing else. Her legs were clad in sheer stockings, and her feet were encased in high heels.

"Not bad," she said, trying to keep the emotion from her voice. "I ... I think we can find something for you to do. Wait here."

She went to the door adjoining the office of her brother, opened it, and with a backward smile went through and closed the foor after her.

Silently, Gil moved across the room to the door and listened.

"... a Greek god," Mari's excited voice was saying.

"Mari, calm down. You're all hot and bothered again. Now, what's so special ..."

"He's ideal ..."

The man grunted. "To you, an ideal man is one who wears pants."

She ignored the sarcasm. "He had an airline job, but he's out of work now, and ..."

"Airline?" the man said. "What airline?"

"He didn't say, but ..."

"The girl was working for an airline. Trans-U.S. Stewardess. Business must be bad for them if they're laying off everybody. It sounds fishy to me."

"Anyway, Edmund," Marie said, "you know the job we can use him on."

"Anyway, Edmund," Mari said, "you know the job we can use him on."

"Yes," Edmund Beaubelle said thoughtfully. "Let me talk to him."

Gil retreated as Mari's footsteps approached the door. He pretended interest in one of the abstract paintings as she came back into the room. He turned to face her.

"Do you have anything for me right away," he asked. "I could really use some work right now."

"There's a job coming up," she said. "My brother Edmund would like to talk to you about it."

"Oh. Is he in the business with you?"

"He's a doctor. He examines our models to make sure they're physically all right to accept jobs. Certain assignments require good physical condition. You can go right in."

"Thanks, I will." Gil hesitated, then flashed Mari a smile. "Will I see you again?"

"After you're through with Edmund," she promised.

He nodded, and went through the door into the other office. The room was very similar to the one he'd just left, except there was another door that was open and leading to what looked like an examination room. Behind the large desk, Edmund Beaubelle looked up, rose, and came forward, smiling, hand extended.

"Mr. Baxter," he said, "I'm Doctor Beaubelle, Mari's brother."

He was a man in his late forties, with a somewhat flabby face partially concealed behind a mustache and short beard connected along either side of the mouth. His hair was sparse, greying, and combed straight back. He was wearing a business suit.

Gil took the hand and shook it. "Glad to meet you, doctor," he said. "Your sister says you have a job for me."

"That depends," Edmund Beaubelle said testily, "on your physical condition, among other things." He returned to his chair behind the desk and indicated that Gil should take the seat in front. "Do you know Charlie Clark very well?"

"No," Gil admitted. "I just talked to him once on the phone, and he invited me out for a drink."

Edmund Beaubelle stroked his heard thoughtfully. "Charlie is a strange person, Baxter. Steeped in the old tradition and afraid of new advances. He tries to act mysterious about things that are not mysterious."

"He did mention a travel club," Gil said.

Beaubelle laughed. "It's one of his pet gripes. In the old days, people sat around the Country Club and acted like the Idle Rich, and Charlie Clark would like a return to those days. The travel club, Baxter, is just that. The reason we're so secretive about it is that we don't want a bunch of tourists descending on us. In fact, the job we have in mind for you concerns the travel club."

"Oh?" Gil said, and waited.

"Yes. Oh, by the way, Mari mentioned you worked for an airline."

Gil nodded. "Trans-U.S. Business was falling off, and they laid off about a dozen of us, pilots, copilots, stewardesses ..."

"Do you know a girl named ..." Edmund Beaubelle frowned in thought ... "Carla O'Brien?"

"Carla O'Brien?" Gil said, as though considering it. "Oh yes, a cute redhead. She was on a few of my flights. Why?"

Beaubelle chuckled. "To coin a phrase, it's a small world. She was in here yesterday looking for a job."

Gil's heart was pounding. He forced his voice to be casual. "Did you hire her?"

"Of course. She's most attractive. If you take the job, you'll probably see her in Mexico. She left late yesterday afternoon."

Gil breathed a sigh of relief. "What sort of work would I be doing down there?"

"Hardly anything at all, really. The job lasts for three days, and you'll be paid three hundred dollars for it. It's mostly a party, and you'll be there for atmosphere, along with Carla and some other good looking men and women."

"That's a lot of money for doing nothing," Gil said.

"That depends on your viewpoint." Edmund Beaubelle pointed out. "Well, that's about it. Mari can give you an advance if you're interested."

"I'm interested," Gil said. "When do I start?"

"Tonight. You'll be picked up about nine o'clock." Beaubelle stood up. "I'll see you when you arrive down there, and give you further instructions."

"Fine," Gil said. "And thanks."

He went across the room to the door leading to Mari's office, and turned as he opened the door to look at Beaubelle. But the doctor had busied himself with some papers on his desk. Gil frowned. There was something fishy, all right. It had been entirely too easy. Hardly any questions about his background, no hedging when it came to Carla's disappearance. Was it possible that everything was really on the up and up?

Or is that what they wanted him to think? There was only one way to find out. He'd have to play along with them, not merely to satisfy his curiosity but to find Carla and make certain she was all right.

More than over, Gil was convinced that something was wrong. They might be using Carla as bait for him. If not, it would be a three-day holiday in Mexico. If so, he would be walking into a trap from which there would be little opportunity for escape!

CHAPTER NINE

As Gil entered her office, Mari looked up expectantly.

"It looks like I've got a job," he said.

"Good," Mari said enthusiastically. "I can give you a one hundred dollar advance now, and the rest later when you finish."

She took a thick envelope from her desk and counted out five twenty-dollar bills, which she handed to Gil. As he took the money, their hand touched and Mari's lingered, the fingers moving in almost a caress. Then she pulled her hand back quickly, obviously, and looked away, but her bosom was rising and falling heavily.

"Is ... is there anything more you'd like to know?"

"Just one thing," he said. "Will you have lunch with me?"

She laughed, pleased. "No wonder you're broke. You like girls!"

"It is a weakness of mine," he admitted, grinning at her. "But I didn't mean anything elaborate. How about a picnic? We can pick up some sandwiches and a bottle of wine and drive to Griffith Park. How does that sound?"

"It sounds ... marvelous," she said. "Let me tell Edmund."

She slipped into the adjoining room, leaving the door ajar this time.

"Edmund, I'm going to lunch with Mr. Baxter. I'll be back in a couple of hours."

"Have fun, but ..." He hesitated, then whispered something that Gil couldn't hear.

"I will," Mari promised.

She returned to the room and took Gil's arm warmly. "You mustn't mind Edmund," she said. "He's an old grouch."

"How could I possible dislike a big brother," Gil said, "who has such a lovely sister?"

Mari smiled, pleased, and pressed herself closely against him as they walked down the corridor. In the elevator, she turned to face him so that her breasts were grazing his chest.

"We can take my car," she said, leading him to the parking lot at the rear of the building.

She handed Gil a set of keys and led him to the blue Thunderbird. He opened the door for her, and as she slipped into the seat, her skirt pulled up to reveal and expanse of tempting white thigh. She didn't appear concerned over the display of flesh.

A nearby liquor store provided a bottle of burgundy wine and an Italian delicatessen furnished two huge torpedo sandwiches.

The sun was warm and comfortable as they went up Wilshire toward Western. Gil was aware that Mari was looking at him with increasing interest. Occasionally, he glanced at her, and he could see the excitement growing in her ... an excitement born of anticipation.

He made the turn on Western and drove up past the girl's school and onto Los Feliz, then into Griffith Park itself. The car accelerated uphill, along the winding, fern-lined road, past an occasional parked car or hiker.

"I'll show you where to go," Mari said. "Just keep right on through the park and on up the hill."

Gil nodded. The car swung up the road, climbing higher and higher, until they had reached the turnoff to the Observatory.

"Left on Valle Vista," Mari directed. And then: "Right at the next curve; there's a small hidden turnoff there."

Following her directions, Gil found a small dirt road that led to a bench above the main road. He drove onto it, braked the car, cut the motor. The ledge was dominated by three tall eucalyptus trees and small evergreens.

"No one can see us here," Mari said, "but we can see everyone that comes up the road."

"Handy," Gil said, "but what's so secret about a picnic."

She smiled at him. "You never can tell," she said. "Now, let's get out and start eating. I'm starved!"

She opened the door and got out. Gil followed her to the rear of the car, where she got a blanket from the trunk.

"You think of everything, don't you?" Gil said, in honest admiration.

She nodded. "I try do. Bring the food."

He brought the food. Mari spread the blanket under one of the big eucalyptus trees and sat down on it. Gil caught a glimpse of creamy thigh and wondered if she'd intended the glimpse. He sat down beside her and handed her a torpedo sandwich from the paper bag.

"I suppose these things are fattening," Mari sighed, peeling back the cellophane the surrounded the elongated sandwich, "but I just can't resist them. Say, where's that wine?"

"Right here, but unless you have a corkscrew we're not going to get any of it."

"You'll find one in the glove compartment."

Gil rose and walked back to the Thunderbird. He looked back to see if Mari were watching him. She wasn't. She was intent on another car which was driving slowly up the mountain road.

Gil opened the glove compartment and took his time about finding the corkscrew. There were gasoline credit card receipts, maps of Southern California and Mexico, a tiny .25 caliber

Browning automatic with a loaded clip, the usual assortment of bric-a-brac, and a corkscrew.

He took the corkscrew and returned to Mari. "Mission accomplished," he announced. "It was clear back in the ..."

Mari put a finger to her lips. She pointed, and his gaze followed the direction of her finger.

"There's a couple down there, they just parked."

Through an opening in the bushes, Gil could see a convertible parked on the dirt road below them. A man and a woman were wasting no time in looking at the scenery. They were wearing bathing suits, their lips were blending in a passionate kiss, and their hands were all over each other. He turned his attention back to Mari.

"Love," he said.

"Sex," she corrected him. "Well, let's get to that wine."

Gil carefully worked the corkscrew into the wine bottle cork, and then placing the bottle between his knees, slowly rocked the cork silently from its position. The savor of wine rose to their nostrils.

Gil offered the bottle to Mari, who took it and tipped it back to take a long swallow.

"Oh, that was good," she said, her eyes sparkling. She handled the bottle back to Gil.

Gil took the bottle and drank from it. The sharp dry flavor of the wine trickled headily down his throat. Involuntarily, his gaze drifted to the couple in the convertible below them. They weren't wearing bathing suits any more, and the sight off what they were doing made him feel very excited. He tore his gaze from them and drank from the bottle again, remembering times he and girls had been together in cars. He wondered if his passion had ever been so great he hadn't checked to see if someone could be watching.

"If wonder if they've been properly introduced," Mari said, smiling tolerantly at the couple in the car.

"At any rate, they've certainly been improperly introduced," Gil said.

"As I suspected, you're a prude," Mari laughed.

"Not me. You know, I think this wine is an aphrodisiac."

"Of course," Mari said. "Now let me have some of it."

She leaned over to take the bottle, and Gil became aware of the gentle, enticing movement of her breasts in the tight black dress. His gaze wandered across her hips and legs, and he forced himself to remember that the reason he was here with Mari was to get information about the travel club and what had happened to Carla. He turned his eyes from her, but they fell on the couple below whose faces were now contorted with desire, their bodies writhing frantically against each other ...

He felt his heart beating swiftly, his breath coming faster. The combination of the wine, the sight of what was happening in the other car, the nearness of Mari—all these were beginning to take effect. He noticed that Mari was watching him, amusement in her eyes.

"I'd like to know more about this job in Mexico," he said.

"Really? Funny, I thought there was something else on your mind."

Gil forced a laugh and shifted uncomfortably on the blanket as Mari moved closer to him.

"Of course," he admitted, "but for all I know you may want to get me down in Mexico for illicit purposes."

It was Mari's turn to laugh. "You are a prude."

"No, just careful."

Her face turned serious. "Well, I think it's time you stopped being so careful and kissed me."

Mari flowed into his arms, her eyes closed, her face uptilted. Her arms went around his waist as she forced her breasts against his chest. She was plainly not in the mood for talking, just then. Gil pulled her close to him and kissed her, warmly, moistly, passionately.

"Oh, Gil," she murmured.

Her body shuddered with an expectant convulsion, and she lay back, pulling him with her. She took his hand and placed it over one of her breasts. His hand tightened against the firm woman's flesh. She squirmed against him, panting now, her fingers busy on his clothing, her dress already pulled up over her hips, her body arching in anticipation.

Gil could feel his pulse racing, his senses expanding beneath her touch, his breath becoming ragged and matching hers. He opened his eyes and saw that her eyes were slitted with passion, showing faintly green and moist-looking.

She let out an animal moan of pleasure and began to gasp excitedly. She pulled his head to hers, their lips combined, their tongues danced. Their bodies moved with increasing passion.

"Oh, Gil!" she cried breathlessly.

She became an animal, with only one thought in mind. Her fingernails raked Gil's back, her body locked about him, her teeth bit into his shoulder. She shouted silent words of passion and excitement.

Gil gripped her shoulders tightly, holding on, feeling the crescendo of passion rising to its inevitable climax. The sensual explosion came, and for a moment all outward movement stopped beneath the whirlwind of sensuality that swept over them.

Then they were lying limp and sweat-soaked, apart from each other on the blanket, gazing up at the gently swaying branches of the eucalyptus and at the cotton clouds racing across the blue sky.

Mari propped herself up on one elbow. "Wow!" she said.

Gil grinned at her. "Agreed," he said.

He remembered wondering if he'd ever been so passionate that he hadn't checked to see if some-were watching. Now, he knew ... and anti-climactically he looked around but could see no one. But then Mari had not given him time. He had wanted to talk to her, really, but her body had demanded his and there was no denying it.

Mari straightened her dress and glanced at her watch. "It's getting late," she said. "We'd better go back."

The convertible on the road below had disappeared. Gil gathered up the blanket, folded it. Mari stood on tiptoe to kiss him lightly on the cheek.

"You're very nice, Gil," Mari said.

"You're not so bad youself," Gil admitted.

They got in the car. "I'd like to stay with you all afternoon," she said, "but Edmund gets nervous if I'm out for any length of time." She squeezed his hand. "We'll see each other in Mexico, though."

"Of course. But I'll be one of the hired hands down there. Will I be allowed to mingle with the guests?"

"It'll be your job to mingle," Mari pointed out. "That's why we hired you."

"And Carla O'Brien?" he said, trying to sound casual about it.

"Same thing," she said.

They started back down the road. Gil wondered just how far the "mingling" was supposed to go.

"You seem awfully interested in this Carla O'Brien," Mari said. "Is she a girl friend of yours?"

Gil shook his head. "No, I'd just met her a couple of times on some flights. She seemed like a nice kid. I'd hate to see anything bad happen to her."

"She's perfectly safe," Mari assured him. "You'll probably see her when you're in Mexico. Did Edmund tell you what time you'd be picked up?"

"He said nine o'clock, but he didn't give me any details. I thought you might fill me in."

"There nothing more you have to know right now," she said. She laughed and touched his hand. "Don't look like we're shanghaiing you, Gil. I's just that we have to protect our guest's privacy. You probably wouldn't tell anyone, but Edmund would never forgive me if I blabbed. Just have faith."

"Okay," Gil said, forcing a grin, "I'll have faith."

It was pretty obvious that Mari wasn't going to tell any secrets, at least just then. There was the possibility that if he forced the issue, she'd get suspicious and not take him to Mexico. He was pretty sure that Carla was really down there, as they both had said, and he'd have to play along with them if he wanted to see her.

It was two o'clock when Gil pulled the blue Thunderbird into the parking lot adjacent to Wilshire Boulevard. He cut the motor and handed Mari the keys.

"Sorry I got you back so late," he said.

"It was business,' she said. "In a sense, you might say I was auditioning you!" She laughed, then her eyes clouded at a sudden thought, and she reached out to touch him arm, gently. "Gil—"

"Yes?"

She shook her head. "Nothing," she said, but her smile was forced. She opened the door. "I'll see you in Mexico."

"In Mexico," he repeated.

He walked her to the entrance of the building, where she squeezed his hand and darted through the front doorway. Gil stood for a moment watching her, then he turned and walked back to his own car.

His thoughts were troubled. Mari's look had told him more than any generality she could have come up with vocally. The look had been a warning, a premonition of danger that lay waiting for him in the untraveled regions of Mexico. More than ever, Gil was certain that there was something about the travel club that was not only phoney but sinister as well.

Carla was undoubtedly alive, as he was now alive. But the question was: for how long?

CHAPTER TEN

It was eight-thirty, and Gil had finished packing. He'd thought again of telephoning the police, but he dismissed it once more. Beaubelle would have all tracks covered, and as far as anyone knew, his operation was a travel club and nothing more. Besides, Carla was in their hands, somewhere in Mexico, and if the game was a dangerous one Edmund would undoubtedly not hesitate getting rid of her. Gil couldn't take the chance.

He made several telephone calls, one of them to Brenda, who was not at home—or else was refusing to answer the phone when he called. She would probably be preparing for the trip herself.

Another call was to Charlie Clark, whom he briefed on the activities of the past day.

"If you don't hear from me in three days," Gil told him, "I think it would be wise to inform the police."

"Okay, Gil," Charlie said. "Be careful boy."

After the call, Gil breathed a minor sigh of relief. It would be nice having someone back in Los Angeles know his whereabouts—just in case. It would guarantee a safe return for him and Carla.

Gil packed a small suitcase, filled mostly with underwear, handkerchiefs and toilet articles. He put in an extra pair of slacks and a sportscoat. Mari had suggested he dress informally, so he was taking her at her word. Sportshirt, slacks, a jacket. There was also an item she didn't suggest, but one which could easily come in handy.

It was a slim Beretta Panther with a full load of nine .25 calibre cartridges in its clip, nestled snuggly in his coat pocket.

Promptly at nine o'clock there was a knock at the door, a single authoritative sound, once like opportunity. Two men stood in the hallway. They were both tall, about six feet one or two and appeared to have been made from the same mold. Each was in his late twenties, had brown, closely-cropped hair, a pleasant look etched on his face. They were both dressed in grey business suits.

"Baxter," one of them said, "we're from the Agency."

"Yes, come in," Gil said.

They walked into the living room, and Gil closed the door behind them. He turned to face them, and gasped. One of them had a .45 automatic in his hand.

"Don't be alarmed, Baxter," the man said. "Just a precaution. We have to search you."

"Now, see here—"

The man shook his head impatiently. "A formality, but we take it very seriously. Some of our guests get strange ideas. They carry weapons with them, and we don't want anyone to get hurt."

Gil wet his lips, which had suddenly become dry. He could feel the weight of the slim Beretta in his pocket and wished he'd hidden it in his suitcase.

"Turn around and face the wall." He smiled. "Please," he added with exaggerated politeness.

Wordlessly, Gil turned and faced the wall. He knew he had no choice in the matter. His best bet was to play along, if he wanted to see Carla.

"That's it. Now lean forward with your hands flat against the wall and your feet back."

Resignedly, Gil assumed the undignified but classic position of a man about to be searched. He felt hands entering his pockets, exploring his armpits, feeling along his trouser legs. A glance told his the other man was doing the searching. The one with the gun was not within vision but he was certainly present, the gun held casually but securely in his hand.

The Beretta was snaked from his coat pocket, and the searcher stepped back.

"All right, Baxter, you can turn around now," the man with the gun said. "Is that your suitcase?" he continued, indicating the bag nearby.

Gil nodded, and the other man went to the suitcase, knelt, opened it and made a fast but thorough search of its contents. He closed it again and stood up, nodding.

"It's okay," he said. He held up the Beretta.

"What about this?" The man shrugged and pocketed his own weapon. "Leave it." To Gil: "Sorry to inconvenience you, but we have our orders. Let me introduce myself. My name is Tom. My companion here is Dick."

Gil had to laugh. "And I suppose Harry is waiting out in the car?"

The man smiled. "As a matter of fact, he is. Shall we go?"

Gil picked up the suitcase, opened the door. The two men preceded him; he took one last look at the apartment, flicked the light switch, and went out.

The night was clear and cool, the sky black and filled with stars. A large black Cadillac sedan was waiting for them at the curb. The man who had introduced himself as Tom went into the driver's seat. A man inside the back seat opened the door for Gil, who got in and sat down. The door slammed behind him.

"You're Harry," Gil said.

"That's right," the man said humorlessly.

He was dressed like the others, and had a pleasant, unobtrusive face it would be difficult to pick out of a crowd.

The Cadillac engine started, and the big car moved away from the curb and accelerated down the street.

Harry was regarding Gil with faint amusement. "What are they going to use this one for?" he wanted to know.

"How should I know?" Dick said. He laughed. "Maybe the pony's sick."

The man behind the wheel shot him a sharp glance.

"You talk to much." To Gil: "You may as well relax, Baxter. We've got a long drive ahead of us."

"Can I ask where we're headed?" Gil said.

"Mexico," the driver said.

"Anywhere in Mexico in particular?"

"We'll let you know when we get there," the driver said. "It shouldn't matter. I understand they pay you guys pretty well for your services."

"Are you supposed to take me back when I've finished?"

"Maybe. They didn't say. They don't tell us a lot of things, and we aren't paid to ask questions. Neither are you, by the way. This is your first time, apparently"

"The first time," Gil agreed.

"Well, I doubt that you're in for a fate worse than death."

"Do you do this often?"

"Do what?"

"Pick up people this way,"

"Sometimes."

It was obvious they weren't going to be talkative, so Gil fell silent and contented himself with looking out the window at the neon storefronts. By tomorrow they would be someplace in Mexico—south of San Felipe, Charlie Clark had said—and he would see Carla again He hadn't realized he could miss anyone so much. Inevitably his thoughts turned to Brenda, and he wondered what she was going to do about the child she was carrying.

He still felt a sense of obligation toward her, but he knew now that it would be a mistake to marry her because of it.

"Cigarette?"

Gil looked to see Harry offering a pack, and shook his head no. The other man paused to light up a cigarette for himself.

"Things aren't so bad," he said. "The cops and robbers routine is sometimes necessary. Mostly, it's a pretty routine job."

"What was that remark about the pony?" Gil said.

Harry laughed, and the driver said quickly, "He was just kidding."

"Yeah, that's right," Harry said, "we're all great kidders. By the way, would you care for a coffee and a sandwich?"

"A coffee would be great," Gil decided. "Black."

Harry reached into a metal box at his feet and brought up a vacuum bottle and some plastic cups. He poured steaming black coffee into a cup and handed it to Gil. He poured two more and handed them to the two men up front, and then passed over two sandwiches. Then he poured himself a cup and sat back, slowly munching on a sandwich himself.

The Cadillac sped along route 99 South toward Mexico. There was little doubt, despite the attempts at secrecy, that they were heading for Mexicali in Mexico, just across the border from Calexico, California. From there, the choice of routes was limited. They could go along route 2 into Mexico proper or continue directly south on route 5 which ended at San Felipe.

Meanwhile, there was nothing Gil could do so he sipped at his coffee and watched the cities become desert outside, and then he closed his eyes and listened to the steady hypnotic hum of the tires against the road.

He dozed, awakening as they passed through Coachella and Brawley. When they reached El Centro, the driver began to outline the plan for crossing the border.

"There's no real inspection going into Mexico," he said. "However, some of the border patrolmen do ask a few questions, now and then, so it's best to be prepared."

He spoke as though to all of them, but Gil knew the words were directed at him.

"Have you been to Mexico before, Baxter?"

"Just to Tijuana a few times," Gil said, "and once to Ensenada."

The driver nodded. "It's roughly the same routine. If anyone asks, you're a tourist going down to look over the country for a few days. This late at night, they sometimes look us over to see that we're not carrying any minors or stolen goods."

"You must be fairly well known at the border," Gil said.

"Yes, I am. In fact, I think they're beginning to wonder why I come down her so often, but since I'm not doing anything illegal they can't do anything." He laughed. "In fact, I'm sure that at least one of them thinks I'm a pimp. He can think what he likes as long as he doesn't interfere with my business."

"Were getting a little low on gas. We're better off getting some gas when we cross the border. It's cheaper."

"I'd like to make a quick trip to the men's room when we stop," Gil said.

"Sure, it's just a few more miles," the driver said.

"How many miles before we get to San Felipe?" Gil asked casually.

"About one hndred twenty-five," the man in the front seat answered automatically, and then he smiled as though realizing he'd given out some information unitentionally.

Gil pretended to take no notice. Besides, his mind was busy with other thoughts. Carefully, he felt outside his pocket to make sure the ball point pen was still there. He would stop in the gas station restroom and scribble a message for Charlie Clark, telling him that they were indeed on their way to San Felipe, as he'd suspected.

They went through the streets of Calexico. For the small hours of the morning, the streets were heavily-trafficked with people coming and going across the border. They made the turn and slowed as they approached the Mexican inspection station. Gil allowed his eyes to roam over the signs telling narcotics addicts to register, saying that animals taken in Mexico can not be returned, etc. While modern in many respects, parts of Mexico were still primitive and unsettled, and once they were beyond the civilized areas, anything could happen.

The car stopped, and a mustached Mexican official in khaki leaned forward to glance in the car. His eyes flicked briefly over the inhabitants, then he grinned faintly, nodded, and waved them on.

The Cadillac moved ahead onto the rough streets of Mexicali, silently, slowly.

"There's a gas station in the next block," the driver said. "You can go to the john there, Baxter."

The car passed a huge Pepsi-Cola sign, a billboard that said, *BIENVENIDOS AMIGOS WELCOME*, past stores that advertised *LICORES* and stores brightly decorated and designed to appeal to the tourist. A large Standard station loomed upon them, and the Cadillac slid silently into the driveway and came to a stop beside the row of pumps.

Gil got out, stretched and yawned. "I'll be right back he said.

"I think I'd better go, too," Harry decided suddenly.

Gil tried to suppress a frown of disappointment, as the man nonchalantly ambled alongside him to the door labeled HOMBRES. He realized with a sinking heart that it was no coincidence that one of the men was accompanying him to the men's room. It was part of the routine. They weren't taking any chances on him trying to send a message to someone.

Gil entered the men's room and went immediately to one of the stalls, closed the door behind him. Pretending to be busy with natural functions, he unrolled several feet of toilet paper, took out his pen and wrote: "Contact Charlie Clark at—" and he wrote down Charlies phone number—" in Los Angeles. Message: *on way to San Felipe; Gil. Important. Money in cyclinder.*" He rolled the paper back up, took the roll down and placed a five-dollar bill in the cylinder and replaced the roll on the wall. Then he got up, flushed the toilet and opened the door.

Harry was leaning against the wall, casually smoking a cigarette. Without a word, he brushed past Gil and went into the stall. Gil noticed that another stall was empty, and Harry did not have to wait unless he'd wanted the one Gil had left. He busied himself at the wash basin, trying to listen for sounds of searching. After a few minutes, Harry came back out without a word, washed his hands, and then went back out to the car.

Gil breathed an inaudible sigh of relief. Apparently, as he'd intended, he'd unrolled enough of the paper to be safe. It was a close call.

The car was serviced and ready to go. Gil climbed in the back seat, and Harry got in from the other side. The car moved off down the road, turned onto route 5 and accelerated rapidly. Ahead of them lay stretches of Mexican desert and little more, and at the end of the road San Felipe. And then what? Gil didn't know, but he felt a little better in knowing that there was a chance Charlie Clark would get his message.

He stared out the window at the distant mountains outlined against the night sky sprinkled with stars.

"You know," Harry mused, "you're pretty naive, Baxter."

Gil stared at him.

"To think," the man elaborated, "that anyone would take your message seriously." He laughed. "The only thing they'd have taken would be your money. Here, better save this for your old age—if you live that long."

In his hand was the five dollar bill Gil had hidden in the restroom!

CHAPTER ELEVEN

The black Cadillac sedan sped through the Mexican desert along route 5, heading south toward San Felipe—and perhaps beyond. Hours passed, and the scenery changed from sparsely vegetated land to mountains to rolling sand dunes. The early morning sky began to glow to their left, beyond a distant range of mountains, and then the sun broke free and flooded the land with light and warmth. The driver touched a button, and air conditioning flooded the car with silent coolness.

No further mention had been made of Gil's attempt to leave a message for Charlie Clark, and Gil wasn t about to make an issue of it. Meekly, he had accepted the fact of his discovery. The message had only been a corroboration anyway. From his nosing around at the Country Club, Charlie had suspected it would be San Felipe this trip, so it would be logical that if Gil didn't show up after three days the man would look in that area for him.

They accelerated up a hill and at its peak there was a sign beside the road that said SAN FELIPE, and beyond it the fishing village itself and the great blue stretch of water that was the Gulf of California. They descended into the village and at the center of town the paved road ended abruptly.

They turned onto the dusty main street and moved slowly past the small wooden and adobe structures that were houses and stores. Signs advertised Mexicali beer and cafes seemed numerous. Gil noticed with amusement that there was even a place that advertised itself as a Chinese restaurant specializing in chow mein.

Boys ran laughing through the streets, and an occasional native looked up at them considering them tourists and then paid no attention as the car continued along the road which was gradually becoming more sandy as they left the town. The car swung up an incline and onto the beach, where it stopped. Ahead of them, a helicopter rested on the sand, the pilot sitting in its shade drinking a bottle of Mexican beer and wiping his forehead with a sleeve. At the sight of the car, he got up, smiled and came to meet them.

"This is the end of the line, Baxter," the driver announced. "For us anyway. Roach will take you the rest of the way."

The man called Roach came up to the car, and Harry pressed a button that lowered the rear window. Instantly, a blast of hot humid air entered the car, overpowering the air conditioning.

"Boy, am I glad to see you fellows," Roach said, showing crooked teeth in a grin of welcome. "It's a hundred thirty out there. Is this my passenger?"

"This is the one, Roach. His name's Baxter, Gil Baxter. Be careful with him."

"Sure," Roach said. "Glad to meet you, Baxter. You're not afraid of flying in a helicopter are you?"

"No," Gil said. He didn't volunteer the information that he was a pilot and had flown helicopters. The thought occured to him his knowledge might just come in handy.

"Well," Roach said, "let's get going."

"Maybe I'll see you fellows on the way back?" Gil said.

"Maybe you will," Tom agreed, but there was no promise in his tone.

Gil got out and closed the door, and the Cadillac turned and moved back down the road to San Felipe.

Roach watched them leave. "Those guys are lucky driving an air-conditioned car."

"Yes," Gil said.

It was hot and muggy, and his clothes were beginning to stick to him uncomfortably. He removed his jacket.

"Can I buy you a beer?" he offered.

"No, thanks," Roach said. "Against the rules. Besides, it'll be cooler where we're going."

Another chance gone to contact Charlie Clark. Gil considered using the excuse that he had to go to the john, then decided there would be no point to it. They climbed aboard the helicopter, and Roach started the great blades chopping the air. Slowly, the machine lifted the ground and rose steadily.

"I understand a friend of mine came down here yesterday," Gil said, above the road of the helicopter. "A girl." He described Carla.

Roach shrugged. "Could be," but he refused to comment further. "The place is just a few miles down the coast. If she's there, you'll see her."

Gil was forced to content himself with that. He looked over the side of the helicopter and watched the sandy stretches of beach pass beneath them. They passed along a small mountain that squatted in the water and headed south. The land was desolate, its naturalness marred only by an occasional adobe hut that looked as though it were unoccupied.

He made no further attempts at conversation. A stretch of mountains and the helicopter fought for altitude, found it, annd dropped gently toward the other side. Roach pointed, and Gil followed the direction of his finger.

Below and ahead of them, nestled in a small valley beside the gulf was a great stone building that resembled in many ways a medival castle. In the center of the huge building was a courtyard, circular and surrounded by elevated rows of stone benches, where Gil surmised they probably held bullfights since it resembled the arenas he'd seen. He noticed that a dirt road snaked from someplace in the mountains and ended at the entrance to the building.

"I never knew this place was here," Gil said.

"Few people do. It's on private property, and the only road leading to it is guarded, in case any curious ones decide to do some exploring."

The helicopter headed for the arena and lowered itself gently to the ground. As the blades slowed, Gil noticed a man was coming to meet them—Edmund Beaubelle. He got out, and the man grinned at him.

"Glad you could make it, Baxter," he said. "No doubt you're tired from your journey and you'd like to rest."

"Not really," Gil said. "I thought I might take a look around."

"You thought wrong," Beaubelle told him. "Come with me. I'll show you to your room."

Gil hesitated, then said, "I'd like to see Carla O'Brien."

Beaubelle was still grinning, but the grin was unpleasant. "I'll bet you would," he said. "I don't blame you. She's a most attractive girl. Although," he went on, "hardly worth getting yourself into a mess over."

Gil stared at him. "What do you mean?"

"Do you take us for idiots, Baxter? We were on to you from the very first. The rooms at the Country Club are wired, and we heard your entire conversation with Charlie Clark."

Gil's heart sank.

"Furthermore, why do you think we didn't bother investigating you. Simply because we knew all we wanted to about you already. We didn't give a damn whether you were here to spy on us or not, because you wouldn't be telling anybody. Make no mistake, Baxter, you're our prisoner here and there's nothing you can do about it, so you may as well relax until we decide just how to kill you. It's a problem, because there are really so many delightful ways."

"You bastard," Gil said, clenching his fists. "Do you have Carla here?"

"Of course," he said. "A pity she, too, will have to die. She's very pretty and has a remarkable figure. She should provide us with some excellent entertainment."

"You Son-of-a-bitch!" Gil said, and he stepped toward Beaubelle.

Unfazed, the doctor made a signalling motion with his hand, and Gil remembered the pilot Roach behind him. He turned quickly, but not before the metal wrench had crashed heavily into the base of his skull and the darkness came.

CHAPTER TWELVE

The window of Gil's cell overlooked the wild Baja California surf. Dashing against the rocks fifty feet below, the waves violently chewed against the rocky foundation and with every crash of the turbulent water, the floor seemed to vibrate.

Consciousness had come slowly. Gil lay on the cell's stone floor, holding his storm-filled head as a pain behind his eyes pounded with each heartbeat. He felt the coldness of the floor and hugged it to him in an effort to shock himself awake. He forced his eyes open and winced at the sharp stripes of light falling brightly on the floor.

He breathed deeply, resting for a moment, and then he rolled over to look at his surroundings. The room was starkly functional, with a cot bolted to one wall, a sink and a toilet in one corner. There was a single window overlooking the gulf, and the window was barred. A bare electric bulb hung from a cord in the ceiling.

The pain was still strong in his head from the blow Roach had given him with the wrench. Straining every aching muscle, he forced himself to a sitting position and then testily rose to his feet. Nausea swept over him as he reached out to a nearby wall to steady him. Then he made his way to the window to look out.

The sun had risen high into the blue sky, and the gulf reflected the blueness in its calm waters. Except the water was not calm where it dashed itself against the rocks below. Even if there were no bars on the window, escape would be difficult.

Wearily, he sank back on the cot, which seemed to envelop him with its comparative softness. Tiredness ebbed through him again and he dozed, and then suddenly he became aware of movement in the room. A deep-reaching musky scent sank into his lungs, and his stomach grew taut again and then subsided. His head was no longer resting on a cot but in the lap of a woman.

Carla, he thought, and opened his eyes.

Mari smiled down at him, "Feeling better?" she asked.

"Yeah, great," he said, "thanks to your brother."

"I'm sorry it had to happen, Gil, really I am. Edmund says he did it in self-defense. Anyway, I have some medicine here for you." Gil noticed she had a glass in her hand, filled half with a colorless liquid. "I promise it'll taste awful, but it will shake the headache."

Submissively, Gil opened his mouth to receive the liquid from the glass Mari held to his lips and discovered she was right about one thing: the mixture in the glass tasted like all the filth in history distilled into one vile liquid. His gorge rose automatically at the first swallow, and then miraculously subsided. Within seconds, his head cleared, and though weak, he suddenly felt better. He tried to sit up, but Mari forced his head back down again.

"Relax for a few minutes," she said, "until your head clears. Edmund may have some nasty moments, but he is a good doctor. Are you hungry?"

"Starving," he said.

"It's a little late for breakfast, but one of the servants is bringing it up in a few minutes. Steak, eggs, all the trimmings."

"A last meal for the condemned man?" he said wrily.

Mari's face clouded. "Don't joke about it," she said.

"Who's joking? I hope your brother Edmund was."

"Let's not talk about it just now." she said. "Let's just enjoy ourselves."

Gil noticed that Mari was wearing only a thin raw silk gown, and that her full breasts were only an inch from his cheek. He was aware that Mari liked him, and he could use a friend right now. He reached out and took her hand.

"What do you suggest?" he said.

She smiled and opened her mouth as though to say something, when a discreet knock came at the door. Mari sighed removed Gil's hand from hers and stood up.

"Come in," she said.

A man in white trousers and shirt came in, pushing a tea cart crowded with covered dishes, china, orange juice, silverware, and a steaming coffee pot. Wordlessly, he pulled a small table from its position by the door and spread a white tablecloth over it. Never looking directly at either Gil or Mari, he set the table for two, poured a single glass of orange juice and left the room.

Gil sat up cautiously. His head was still light with hunger, but the terrible pain was gone. His muscles ached vaguely, but with none of the bone-breaking fatigue he had known earlier. He smiled and reached out for Mari.

"Shall we continue our discussion?"

"Later," she said. "Your breakfast will get cold. I never do."

Mari sat beside him on the cot and uncovered the dishes to reveal blood-rare steaks sizzling still, several eggs, fried potatoes. Deftly she transferred these to the plate in front of Gil.

Gil watched her movements, wondering how she could be so calmly domestic with a man her brother had sworn to kill. He wanted to ask her about Carla, but he felt instinctively this would not be a good time. If he wanted her for his friend, his thoughts and actions should seem for her alone; he'd already experienced the antics of jealous women a few times too often.

She poured two cups of coffee, took one for herself. Gil busied himself with the food, which was very good, while she sat and watched him silently. He could feel her eyes on him, devouring him hungrily. When he'd finished, he sighed, leaned back and slowly sipped his coffee.

"That was very good," he said. "Do you always feed your prisoners this well?"

"You're not a prisoner," she said. "At least, you're not confined to this room; the door's open. You must let me show you around."

"I'd love it," he said, honestly. In order to escape, he'd have to know the layout of the place. "I never knew this place was down here."

"Hardly anyone does. It was built many years ago by Jose Romanceno, the silent film star, to certain specifications. After he faded out of the picture business, he retired here and died a few years ago. Edmund picked it up for a song, and we've been using it a lot for the travel club."

"Doesn't it get monotonous coming to the same place all the time?"

Mari smiled inscrutably. "No one has complained yet," she said. "I'll give you the guided tour, and perhaps you'll see why."

Gil gulped down the rest of his coffee. "I'm ready whenever you are."

"Let's go, then."

They stood up, and Mari led the way through the door into a corridor, down a flight of winding stairs. At the foot of the stairs there was another corridor, and she led him to one of the doors, opened it, and motioned for him to enter.

It was a large room, ornately furnished, with a window overlooking what seemed like a brilliant tropical garden. There was a dressing table with a large mirror, and in one corner of the room a huge circular bed.

Suddenly his eyes were riveted to the mural on the wall. A man and two women were graphically involved in a gross form of sexual embrace. Slightly stunned, Gil swung his eyes to the next set of figures, which pictured still another variation on the age-old theme. A spark of recognition kindled in his mind—Pompeii. He'd once taken a tour of the city, and the guide had shown him through one of the classical bordellos, where murals displayed a catalog of intricate sexual embraces.

He turned to Mari, who was frankly grinning with amusement. "Delightful aren't they?"

"Very interesting," he agreed. "Is this your room?"

She nodded.

He grinned. "You count positions instead of sheep?"

"You might say that. It always amazes me that people can make the most simple and delightful acts complicated." She stood very close to him, and he could feel the warmth of her breasts even through the thin material she was wearing. "How do you feel?"

"Fine," he said.

His head was perfectly clear, and the ache had gone from his body. Except another ache was beginning to start, a pleasant one associated with Mari's closeness. He thought of Carla and forced himself to move away to the window to look out.

"I'd like to see more of the place," he said.

He turned to see Mari pouting. It was obvious she'd hoped to stay awhile longer in the bedroom. Ordinarily, Gil wouldn't have minded, but Edmund Beaubelle had threatened to kill him, and he had to find Carla and make plans for their escape.

"All right," she said reluctantly, "come on, I'll give you the guided tour.

She led the way through the doorway and back out into a long door-lined hallway. The doors were closed, and Gil fancied he could hear sounds of sighing and moaning and the tossing of bodies, but he considered that it might have been his imagination. It was certainly easy to imagine such things. A series or Aztec religious rituals were painted on the hallway walls, between the doors. The pictures were colorful and uninhibited. Feather-helmeted priests poised ceremonial daggers over the pulsing breasts of naked Indian virgins.

"The art." Mari elaborated, "is a mixture of many cultures, Aztec, Pompeii. And wait till you see some of the other things around here—particularly some of the Polynesian and African primitives. It's a hodgepodge, collected from over the world—but with only two themes, sex and bloodshed. Come on, let me show you the rest of the place."

She led him down a stairway to the next floor. The place was laid out in such a manner that an unwary wanderer would soon find himself lost in a maze of corridors if he weren't careful.

Paintings were hung on the walls of this floor. Works by old and new masters and hacks appeared side by side. All of the paintings had erotic themes, and at least five different versions of "Leda and the Swan" were in evidence.

They continued on down the corridor, and Mari threw open a door. Gil gasped as the sudden sunlight and the brilliance of the tropical garden struck his eyes. Lush green vegetation, trees and bushes of red and gold, and the soft multi-hued richness of millions of flowers rushed in to overwhelm his sense. It was a tropical Garden of Eden.

Stepping into the garden, Gil and Mari moved slowly down the gravel path as Gil admired the scenery.

"You like it?" Mari asked.

"It's magnificent," Gil said honestly.

Stone satyrs pursued stone nymphs beneath bushes. African and Polynesian fertility figures displayed huge genitals and monstrous mammaries while peering at passers-by from half-hidden spots in the foilage. There were small nooks, arbors, bowers and benches set in odd corners and hidden by vines and flowers, apparently for lovers to meet in secret rendezvous.

Mari raised a finger to her lips. "Wait here," she whispered.

She walked carefully up the path, making no sound, then disappeared around a turn in the path. Gil stood waiting, wondering what marvel would occur next. His nostrils flared delighted with the overpowering perfumes of the flowers. The late afternoon heat was beginning to dissipate, and the steady buzz of insects in the silence gave a feeling of relaxed decadence.

Mari appeared again, her finger to her lips once more, and motioned him to come ahead. She indicated a hidden pathway and led him down it. The path led behind a screened bower where Gil could see two people, a man and a woman in a passionate embrace.

It reminded Gil of the time he and Mari had been in the Hollywood Hills observing a couple behaving in similar fashion. He shook his head and pulled away.

"Mari, really—"

"No," she whispered. "This will hold a particular interest for you, Gil."

Gil frowned, but his curiosity was intrigued. He looked.

The man was large and beefy, and the girl was a shapely blonde. They were entwined on a wide bench, lost to the world in a deep lingering kiss. The man was half-sitting on the bench turned toward the girl whose blouse was unbuttoned to expose her breasts. His large hands bruised and manhandled the breasts and then passed down to tear at the buttons of her skirt.

Her legs were drawn up, long and lovely, and the man in his haste ripped one of the buttons and finally worked the other one loose and fumbled at the zipper. The girl shifted her position to give greater access to the bottons and the zipper and as they were freed raised her hips to facilitate removal of the skirt. She sat up briefly and dropped her hands to her side, and with a shrug the blouse was lying on the grass beneath them.

Gil stood transfixed at the sight before him, and he must have uttered a sound because the girl took her lips from the man and looked in Gil's direction. She saw him watching her and smiled and then pulled the man's head down into the valley of her breasts and began busying herself on the man's clothing. Then she pushed him aside and shifted her position ...

Gil turned away, feeling sick and nauseous. Mari walked with him up the gravel path.

"It's an education, isn't it?" she said finally.

"Yes," he said, finding his voice, "yes, it certainly is."

He felt like a fool, and he was sick with the knowledge that he had been a fool. Gil was not a prude, and everything the man and woman were doing and were going to do he had done and would do again.

But the man and the woman making love on the bench had been people familiar to him, and the sight of them together had not been pleasant.

The man was the bulldog-faced guard at the country club, whom Mari had called Harvey.

The woman was Gil's fiancee, Brenda Hamilton!

CHAPTER THIRTEEN

The path that Gil and Mari followed threaded its way through arbors of roses to a temple of Venus in the center of the garden. Tall white columns supported a golden cupola, and a low fountain gurgled in its shade.

"I can't believe it," Gil said, stunned. "Brenda and that ape, making love out in public."

"Nevertheless it's true," Mari said, not unkindly. "Brenda likes to act the professional virgin back in the States, but here she's our most active member. I'm sorry if the knowledge hurts you, Gil, but ..."

She stared at him, puzzled, as he broke out laughing. "It's marvelous," he said, "just marvelous. Mari, you don't know how relieved I am. Originally, I was worried about sweet little Brenda getting in trouble down here, but I see she can take care of herself."

"And now," Mari said testily, "you're worried about Carla."

Gil's heart leaped at the mention of her name, and he opened his mouth to ask where she was.

"First things first," Mari said, before he could speak. "I want to enjoy you before any of the others do."

Gil frowned. "You've been making all sorts of innuendos, but I still don't know why I'm here. Am I supposed to be a gigolo, a model, an actor, a stud—or what? In short, just why did you bring me all the way down to Mexico?"

She hesitated, her face suddenly clouded. "I ... I'd still prefer to not tell you about it, just now anyway. But I'd suggest you save your strength. You'll need it." She forced a smile. "Now, let's go on with our tour, shall we?"

She walked on before he could protest, so Gil followed her up the steps to a temple-like structure elevated above a sea of flowers and lush tropical greens. He could hear the rushing sound of the sea beyond the wall.

"This was where Romancero used to entertain the girls he brought down to Mexico for parties. He was an exhibitionist. He used to gather all his guests and have them watch while he did his stuff."

"It seems to be catching," Gil said, remembering Harvey and Brenda's performance on the bench. Brenda had looked up and seen him, and she hadn't cared that he was watching her. In fact, she'd even smiled as though delighted by his observance.

"That's why the people come down here, Gil. As you suspected, it's not really a travel club. It's a Lust Club. For a fee, we supply thrills to the jaded tastes of the country club set who have everything but the imagination to seek out thrills for themselves." She shrugged. "There's really nothing wrong with it, I suppose. People have to have variations on sex. I have no real objection to the abortions, or the narcotics ..." her voice grew softer and more intense "... but the murders ..."

"Murders?" Gil said abruptly.

He took her arms tightly in his hands and pulled her close to him.

"What murders, Mari?"

She looked up into his eyes, her face suddenly like a frightened child. "Edmund says I talk too much. He's even threatened to kill me at times. He says it's dangerous to have me around. Gil, please, let's get away from here. Edmund is planning on killing you. He's probably watching us right now. I've got money. We can go away someplace in the world where he'll never find me."

A sudden sound in the bushes made her put a hand to her mouth, her eyes widen in fright.

"Hold me, Gil," she told him. "Kiss me, pretend we've no thought but each other."

Her arms clung about his neck, as she pressed herself against him and covered his lips with her own. Gil responded, the pretense almost forgotten with the passion of her embrace and his own reaction to it. He felt her firm full breasts moving against his chest, and his hand drifted down to the lovely feminine buttocks and pressed her slowly grinding hips closer to him.

"Gil, oh Gil," Mari spoke into his mouth, the fires of passion rising in her despite her fear.

There was a movement, and Gil opened his eyes and caught a glance of a girl running naked past them, laughing, followed by a man, also naked, also laughing, running after her. The girl had long black hair and a thin sensuous face, and Gil recognized her as the girl he'd met in the bar who had tried to have him killed or at least hurt in the street. He knew now that she'd been a plant, that she'd followed him into the bar and then lured him outside. He'd been snooping around the travel club's activities, and Baubelle had wanted him taken care of.

"Oh, Gil, we've got to stop."

Gil reluctantly loosened his grasp on her, and she reluctantly pulled away. Reminded of the presence of prying eyes, he felt his excitement fade away. Mari took his hand and led him back down the steps into the shade of the garden.

"We've got to go back in," she said. "The other guests will be arriving soon, and I want to show you a few more things."

"Does everyone arrive by helicopter?" Gil wanted to know.

"No. Many of them drive down here, even though the roads out of San Felipe are not good. In fact, they're hard-packed sand

and dirt, except for the shoulders. If you go off the road, you can't get any traction and your wheels just dig a hole for the car."

"Where do they park the cars?"

"Under the arena," she said.

"And the helicopter?"

"There, too."

Back in the great mansion, Mari took him down a long hall, where she opened a door. The two of them stepped out on what seemed to be a low balcony. Before them stretched the ampitheatre where the helicopter had landed.

"You have bullfights here?" Gil asked.

"Sometimes," she said. "In fact …" she hesitated, then went on, "In fact, we have a bull in the pens right now. Would you like to see him?"

"Yes," Gil said.

Mari motioned for him to follow, and they went out into the corridor again and through another door onto the hard-packed floor of a room that smelled of hay and the sweat of animals. There was a great crashing sound and Gil looked over into a corner, where a large black monster of a bull with gleaming pointed horns was throwing himself at the iron bars of his cage.

Gil whistled in appreciation. "He looks like a mean one."

Mari nodded. "He is. His name is El Diablo—the Devil—and it's a name he deserves." She took his arm. "Let's get out of here, Gil."

"Fine idea," Gil said. "How do you get to the garage?"

"I needn't think you'd have to concern yourself with that, Baxter," a male voice said behind them.

"Edmund!" Mari said.

Edmund Beaubelle's bearded face was twisted into a grimace of a smile. He had a .45 automatic in one hand.

"I think, Mari, you've given Mr. Baxter entirely too much of a tour already. We'd best take him back to his room before he tires. The guests are beginning to arrive, and we have an opening spectacle for them this evening under the arena floodlights."

"I'll take him back," Mari offered.

"No, I think I'll do it, Mari."

He made a motion with the gun, and Gil moved back into the corridor. Beaubelle directed him along the intricate path leading to his cell.

"Who does all the work around here?" Gil asked.

"Servants," Beaubelle answered easily. "They're addicts. They work in exchange for food, lodging, and dope. Ah, here's your room."

It was the cell where he had awakened earlier in the morning. He went in and turned, but Beaubelle had slammed the door behind him. A bolt clicked into place, and Beaubelle grinned at him through a small, barred opening in the door.

"I'd like to see Carla," Gil said.

"It seems we've had this conversation before," Beaubelle said. "Let me remind you, Baxter, that I'm in charge here, and you'll see Carla O'Brien when and if I choose. And right at this moment, I don't choose. I'd rather have you guess the horrible things we're doing to her."

Gil clenched his fists helplessly. "You bastard!"

But Beaubelle only laughed and walked away. Gil listened to the sound of the man's footsteps retreating, and then there was silence. Gil turned back to examine his prison more carefully.

A plain, simple cell that had probably been something else originally. The plumbing had been added later, if broken rock in the wall and cracks in the floor offered any evidence. He walked to the bed bolted to the wall, ran his hand over it, tested it. It was firmly attached.

He got up and went to the barred window looking out onto the gulf. The water, once sky-blue, was turning a muddy color as the sky darkened and the sun set on the other side of the building. A small boat was riding anchor out in the gulf, and it had turned its lights on. Someone on the boat walked in front of a light, blocking it temporarily, and the effect was like a signal.

"Of course," Gil breathed.

He turned on the single bare bulb in the cell, and the dimness of the room faded before the sudden brilliance. The people on the boat might be guests of the thrill club, but they might also be fishermen and perhaps one of them would know International Morse Code. He ripped the blanket from the cot and held it in front of the window.

He hesitated. If Beaubelle knew what he was doing, the man might kill him right away instead of waiting. Then, he began.

He started with a simple SOS, the way he'd learned in the navy ten years before, and followed it with his name and a request for a reply. Then he did it again, and was startled to hear a feminine laugh from the door.

He turned in surprise.

"Brenda!" he said.

"Oh, Gil," she said, through the barred window, "if only you knew how funny you look doing a little dance with that blanket of yours."

"I was—er—just exercising," he said lamely.

"You never were a good liar," she said. "You were trying to signal the yacht out in the gulf. Not that it would do you any good—they're on our side."

"Our side?" he questioned.

"The side of the thrill club, of course," she said, matter-of-factly. "I'm sure you know all about us, by now. I think

I'll always remember the look on your face when you saw Harvey and me doing what comes naturally."

"I was in love with you once, Brenda," Gil said softly.

"Oh, Gil, really!" she said, grimacing her disgust. "Let's not get sloppy. It was laughs, but nothing more."

"Are you pregnant, Brenda?"

She laughed. "Thank goodness, no. I'd hate to go through another abortion, so I had Dr. Beaubelle fix me so I can't have children. No, Gil, there was something glamorous and romantic about going with an airline pilot, so I strung you along. At least," she amended, "I'd thought it was romantic, until you kept bringing up the marriage bit all the time. It's probably just as well you found out about the club."

"Now what?"

"Now you're going to furnish us with some entertainment out in the arena. You remember the old Roman gladiators. Well, that's what you're going to be, Gil, a gladiator. Maybe they'll put you unarmed in the arena with a dope addict who has a knife and the knowledge that if he kills you he'll get some of the stuff he craves."

"Do you know where Carla is?" he asked her.

She smiled. "The women get some pretty special treatment," she said, almost as though to herself, remembering. "Once, we had one manacled to the ground, stripped naked, and cream was poured over her. Then they released twenty hungry cats to go out and lick her. That was fun. She screamed for an hour before she finally died of shock. Then there's the bit wth the Shetland pony ..."

"Brenda, why are you doing this?" Gil said helplessly.

"Because it's thrills, it's kicks, it's fun that not everybody can experience."

"It's vicious!"

"Yes," she said. "Did you know that in ancient Rome where they had the gladiatorial combats, the viewers got worked up to such a frenzy they had sex right in the stands while the blood was flowing in the arena. It's the same way here, Gil. The sight of a bullfight will even do it. The viewer's blood starts pounding in his veins, his heart beats faster, his nerves start to scream for release from the tension—and sex relieves it all."

"I see," Gil said slowly. "When do the contests begin?"

"Tonight," she said, and there was a gleam of anticipation in her eyes.

Gil sighed. "Well, I may as well relax. Wish I had a radio, though, to hear some music."

"I've got a small radio in my room," she said. "I think it'll fit through the bars here."

"I'd appreciate it."

"Sure, Gil, it's the least I can do for you. Don't go away."

She went down the corridor and returned in a few minutes. It was a small white plastic radio that just made it between the bars of the door window.

"Brenda," Gil said, making one last effort, "help me escape."

She shook her head with a determined finality. "No, Gil, I like the club—and I don't want anything to happen to it. It's people like you and Charlie Clark—the nosey ones who won't mind their own business—that deserve what they get. I'm glad it happened to him."

Gil stared at her. "What did you say?"

"Oh, didn't you know? Charlie Clark was killed. Run over by a car." She smiled pleasantly. "It was an accident!"

CHAPTER FOURTEEN

It was several minutes after Brenda had left before Gil could resign himself to the fact that Charlie Clark was dead. An accident, Brenda said. He wondered if his own death would be listed as an accident. More likely, it would be a disappearance, and perhaps there would be a cursory investigation and that would be it—and the Beaubelle's and their lust club would go on.

He had hoped Charlie would alert the American and Mexican authorities, but it looked like the Beaubelles had gotten to Charlie first. And so that was that.

Well, not quite. Not while he still had a breath in his body, anyway.

He turned the small plastic radio over in his hands, wishing it were a transmitter instead of a receiver. But even in code school in the navy they hadn't taught him how to perform magic. Sighing, he plugged the radio into the wall outlet under the bed and turned on. It warmed up, and a Mexican station came in with a torrent of Spanish. As he moved the dial, he could hear other stations coming in faintly. He tuned in KFSD in San Diego and held his ear close to the speaker to hear it. A news program came on, and he listened attentively to hear if his or Carla's disappearance might be mentioned. It was a vain hope.

After a half hour, he turned off the radio and decided Brenda had not told anyone about his attempts to signal anyone in the gulf. He picked up the blanket and looked out the window.

In the darkness of evening, the water had blended with the sky, and the yacht lights seemed suspended in space.

Gil hesitated, knowing his chances were slim. If Brenda were right and the yacht was friendly to the Beaubelle's, the signals would be a useless gesture. But at least it was a gesture, and maybe—just maybe—it wasn't their yacht or maybe there was another boat out farther or someone fishing off a nearby peninsula.

Well, there was no point just standing there. He raised the blanket over the window, blocking the light to the outside, and then he began his signals as before.

Nervously, he kept glancing at the door, half expecting the door to burst open with Edmund Beaubelle waving a gun at him and telling him that his signals had been intercepted. The longer he could prevent this, the better the possibility of his survival. If only Charlie Clark were not dead, and he or someone was out there looking for a signal.

But there was no one waiting. No one.

Twenty minutes passed, and Gil's arms were beginning to feel like lead. The door to his cell crashed open suddenly, and he turned to see Edmund Beaubelle standing in the doorway, his bearded face a mask of fury. The gun in his hand exploded in a burst of sound, and Gil recoiled as the bullet plowed into the wall inches from his head. It was an intentional miss. At the close range, a man with a gun could do much better.

Beaubelle stepped into the room. "You're very clever, Baxter. It's a shame to kill such a talent, but you're too dangerous to be left alive." He made a motion with the gun. "Come along. We've got the entertainment all planned."

Gil rose and silently walked from the room ahead of Beaubelle, who followed him at a discreet distance. They went through the maze of corridors, and Gil's mind was alive with frantic thoughts for escape. He might be able to jump the man, except the doctor knew how to handle a gun—and he'd be able to do Carla no good dead.

"What sort of 'entertainment' do you have planned?" he asked.

"You'll see," Beaubelle promised. "Perhaps much sooner than you wish. You're going to have a fight on your hands, Baxter, such as you've never had before. Ah, here we are."

They paused before a large door at one end of the corridor, and at a signal from Beaubelle, Gil opened it. The door led to the dirt arena, which was dimly lit along the benches but enough for Gil to see that about a hundred people were gathered, mostly in groups of two, around the circumference of the ring.

Gil felt the gun jab his back, and Beaubelle's harsh voice: "Take off your clothes, Baxter. You're going to fight naked. The ladies like it better that way, and we can see the results of the fight more clearly."

Gil hesitated only slightly. The look on Beaubelle's face told him that the man would really hate to shoot him—but he would if he had to, perhaps just a wound here and perhaps another one there. He removed his clothing.

"Very good, Baxter. Now, I want you to understand that I'm a fair man. If you win the fight, I'll give you freedom—and a prize as well."

"A life membership in the country club?" Gil said wrily.

Beaubelle smiled tolerantly. "Something much better than that." He pointed toward the arena, "Look."

Overhead lights flared, bathing the floor of the arena with a daylight brilliance. Gil gasped. In the center of the arena was a six-foot pole imbedded in the hard ground, and tied to the pole was Carla, her naked body gleaming whitely in the lights.

"There is your prize," Beaubelle said, "if you win. If not, your opponent gets her."

"Who IS my opponent?"

Beaubelle motioned with the gun. "Go out there and find out, Baxter. I'd suggest you get there fast, before your opponent gets to your girl."

Laughing, Beaubelle slammed the door shut, and there was the click of a bolt slamming into place.

Resignedly, Gil turned to the arena, and as he walked into the light a murmur rose from the crowd. He paid it no attention. Instead, he went directly to Carla.

"Oh, Gil, Gil, Gil," she sighed. "Thank heaven you are safe."

"Carla, darling," Gil said, kissing her. "I was afraid I'd lost you. Here, let me get these ropes off you."

He fumbled with the ropes, cursing at them for being so secure.

"What are they planning for us, Gil?"

"They're sending someone out to fight me," Gil said. "Probably a dope addict fearing withdrawal—and probably armed as well. Don't worry, though. I'll be fighting for us both, and ..."

A cry of horror tore from Carla's throat. At the same time, the crowd rose to its feet with an excited roar. Somewhere in the audience, a woman screamed.

Gil looked up, and his heart seemed to stop. The hackles on the back of his neck rose. His breath ceased. An intense cold gripped his body, numbing him.

A door had opened, and his opponent had entered the arena and was standing fifty feet away looking at them, its head lowered, hoofs pawing the ground, nostrils flaring, great shiny horns glinting sharply—hundreds of pounds of angry killer bull preparing to charge and destroy. It was the huge bull Gil had seen earlier in the pens.

El Diablo!

CHAPTER FIFTEEN

For a moment Gil stood transfixed hardly daring to believe his eyes. And then he laughed hollowly at the sheer absurdity of the situation. Edmund Beaubelle had promised to be fair. What was fair about a naked, unarmed man fighting a monstrous angry bull?

El Diablo, sharp-horned head lowered, eyes gleaming with the fires of hell, tail flicking nervously, pawed at the ground in front of him. It was no hesitation, but a deliberate surveyal of his victim.

"Gil, run!" Carla cried. "Save yourself."

Her words stirred him into action, and he worked feverishly at the knots securing her to the wooden pole. But the knots were small and tight, and his fingernails couldn't move the strands of rope. The crowd was waiting breathlessly. Suddenly, Carla gasped, and Gil looked up to see El Diablo charging toward them, horns lowered, its feet rumbling hollowly against the dirt floor of the arena.

With a curse, Gil forgot the ropes and ran out to meet the bull. Fear was a cotton rag in his mouth, but he forced himself to run, yelling, hoping to distract the animal's attention. At the last second, he threw himself out of the path of the beast, feeling the dust of it swirling about him, and fell heavily to the ground, rolled, got up quickly in a half crouch.

El Diablo had stopped, puzzled and was looking around at the naked man who had flaunted his body like an insolent cape in front of him. The bull turned around, snorted, pawed the ground again.

Gil looked around at the spectators, shading his eyes in order to see the dim forms of the men and women who had come to get their thrills this way. The wall surrounding the arena was six feet high, designed to protect the onlookers from the bulls—and probably also to prevent any victims from escaping from the arena.

Someone in the crowd shouted "Ole!" and the crowd laughed in nervous response. But Gil knew it was not a contest he was in. A matador had a sword and a cape, and he had helpers who could come to his aid in case of trouble, and he had parts of the bullring where he could seek refuge if need be. Gil had none of this, only a desperate need to survive—and not much chance to. Beaubelle knew there was no chance of him coming out alive, and this was the way it had been planned.

"Gil!" Carla shouted.

The crowd roared again.

El Diablo came at him like a thundering express train. Gil ran, feeling the beast's hot breath on him, and threw himself to one side—not quickly enough. He felt the sharp tip of the horn touch his skin, enter it like a hot needle, tear along the flesh of his arm and come free in a torrent of blood.

The bull went charging past, while Gil rolled away in the dust, feeling the pain of the wound in his arm, sensing rather than hearing the shrieks and applause of the crowd, feeling sick with the knowledge that many of them were happy that blood had been drawn and were applauding the bull.

He staggered to his feet and ran across to a position away from Carla. He felt weak, not so much from the loss of blood, but from the effort of trying to get away from the horned monster which had been sent to destroy him. It wouldn't take much more, possibly only one more charge and he would be impaled on those sharp horns, tossed like a limp rag into the air, and perhaps trampled into the dust for good measure.

And then the beast would turn on Carla and batter and tear her naked body into a bloody pulp!

Wearily, he watched the bull. El Diablo seemed cautious and yet sure of himself. He snorted and pawed the ground.

"No, Gil, no. Edmund stop it!" a female voice—Mari's—cried from the crowd.

Gil glanced in the direction of the voice, a place in the grandstand near the end of the arena. If Carla weren't there he would chance a run across the arena to where Edmund Beaubelle was, he would climb the wall, and take Edmund apart and feed the pieces to the bull.

He sighed. It was a vain dream. Te turned his attention to the bull.

El Diable seemed undecided. He glanced at Gil, and then he glanced at Carla, as though trying to make up his mind. Gil's heart sank. If the bull decided to go after Carla, there was nothing he could do. He yelled at the bull and jumped up and down although the pain in his arm increased with the movements. He came closer.

El Diablo decided. He decided he would take care of the easy one first, and leave the yelling, jumping jack for later.

He lowered his head toward Carla and began his charge.

With a cry, Gil ran to Carla and threw himself in front of her.

"No, Gil, no!" she cried. "Save yourself!"

There was a sharp crack, like the snapping of a giant twig, and the sound of a bullet striking. The crowd got to its feet with an excited murmur. El Diablo paused and considered the round hole in its shoulder and the dark blood flowing from the hole.

There was another shot, and the bull lurched heavily to the ground.

The crowd panicked. Flashlights appeared suddenly all around the perimeter of the arena, and a megaphone voice told everyone it was the police and they were to remain where they were if they didn't want to get hurt. The order was repeated in Spanish.

Gil looked up, dazed by the onset of what was happening.

"Gil," a voice was calling his name.

A familiar figure came running across the arena toward him. The man clasped him by the shoulders.

"Murphy," Gil said, puzzled. "Boy, am I glad to see you. But ..."

"Explanations later, Gil. Let's get Carla out of here."

"You take care of her," Gil said determinedly. "I've got something to do."

"Wait," Murphy said, "I'll go with you."

But Gil wasn't waiting. He raced off in the direction of Mari's voice, reached the wall, leaped, hooked his fingers on the edge of the wall. His left arm came alive with renewed pain, and he winced but held on and pulled himself up and over.

Panting from the effort, he paused only long enough to see the open door leading away from the arena. He raced through it and down the corridor. He glanced behind him at a sound and saw Murphy clambering over the wall. Ahead, he could hear the sound of a car engine roaring into life. He reached the end of the corridor, yanked open the door.

It was the garage, and there were about thirty cars parked in neat rows and the helicopter sitting in one corner. One of the cars was moving, a large black Cadillac sedan, picking up speed as it swung across the concrete floor toward a large open door that showed the blackness of Mexican night beyond it. He caught a glimpse of Edmund at the wheel, with Mari beside him look back, and then the car was outside, heading for freedom.

Murphy came up beside him, panting. "Gil, you're out of your mind. That arm of yours needs attention."

Gil shook his head impatiently. "No time. We can't let them get away." He jerked his head toward the corner. "The helicopter. Quick!"

They raced across the concrete floor. Murphy got into the pilot's seat before Gil could protest, but Gil was grateful for the Irishman's help. His arm was beginning to throb as Murphy helped him into the second seat.

Murphy started the engine, and the huge blades whirled into motion. He touched the controls, and the machine rose slightly.

"Careful of the roof," Gil shouted.

Murphy nodded, and expertly guided the helicopter along the garage a few inches above the ground. They approached the black hole of the door and burst through it into the night. Murphy pulled at the controls, and the machine soared in a steep climb upward.

Gil touched Murphy's arm and pointed ahead of them, on the road below, where the twin cones of the Cadillac's lights swept the darkness. Undoubtedly, Beaubelle knew the road, but fortunately not well enough to travel it without lights. Mari had said it was packed dirt and sand, with soft shoulders. A car could go too near the edge and become stuck, or worse, flip over.

The helicopter roared through the night under full power, heading for the speeding car. Gil became aware of a throbbing in his arm and felt a weakness and the dampness of blood beginning to trickle down his side. His vision blurred, and he shook his head and fought for consciousness.

The Cadillac disappeared behind a turn in the protection of a series of hills, and the helicopter seemed to leap forward with renewed determination. Beneath them, a small lighted yacht was anchored in the gulf. Beaubelle's car was climbing into the hills, along a road bordering the cliff. Gil peered desperately into the darkness. Suppose there was a side road and the man turned off it and doused his lights? They might never find him. It was important that they find him, because a score had to be settled.

Suddenly, they were over the rim of a hill and the Cadillac was directly below them.

Murphy smiled grimly. "Here we go. Hang on!"

He accelerated ahead of the car and dropped down with a sickening whoosh to a spot about ten feet over the road and flicked on his landing lights. The glare was sudden, and Gil was surprised to see the black Cadillac bearing down on them from a point fifty feet away.

He could see two figures in the front seat, and he could imagine the surprised, fearful look on Beaubelle's face as they appeared like an apparition in his path. The car swerved, fish-tailing crazily, then corrected its dangerous path and shot like a bullet under them.

Murphy pulled on the controls, and the helicopter rose, turned, shot after the car. Beaubelle was going too fast to be safe. Suddenly, the car started swerving again, its horn honking frantically. Gil was puzzled, and then he understood. Apparently Maris was trying to convince Edmund that he should stop and surrender, and Edmund was trying to shut her up.

The helicopter lights flashed over the car, and Gil stared in disbelief as the car door opened and a white-gowned figure was pushed, arms flailing, out of the car and into the road.

"Mari!" he gasped. "Forget Edmund, we've got to help her."

Murphy nodded agreement, and banked the helicopter in for a landing on the dirt road, within a dozen yards of Mari's sprawled, silent figure. Gil got out and ran to her, knelt beside her and took her hand to see if there was a pulse. At his touch, she opened her eyes and smiled at him. She tried to sit up and winced.

"Take it easy, Mari," Gil said. "You'll be all right."

"Sure, Gil," she said, "Sure, I will. I knew you'd come after me."

Through the thin material of torn and dirty dress he could see her body was bruised from the fall.

"Gil," she said, "Gil, will you do me a favor?"

"Of course," he said.

She smiled up at him. "Make love to me," she said.

CHAPTER SIXTEEN

"How's the arm?" Murphy wanted to know.

"Not bad, thanks," Gil said, glancing down at his arm swathed in bandages.

It was the following morning in San Diego, with the warm California sun coming in through the window of the hospital and bouncing off the walls and the snow white sheets of his bed. He'd asked the nurse what had happened, but she didn't know. He asked Murphy.

"Mari is pretty banged up, but she'll be all right. Her brother Edmund didn't do so well, though. He lost control of the car after he threw Mari out, and the car skidded and went over the cliff and bounced all the way down to the water." He made a face. "It wasn't pretty."

"I still don't understand how you managed to arrive when you did," Gil said.

"Nothing to it, my boy. It seems that Carla has more faith in me than you. Before she went to the Beaubelles she alerted me to the possibility of monkey business going on. Then, when the two of you disappeared, I figured you must be someplace south of San Felipe so I went down there, discovered your hideaway, and waited for a word or a signal of some kind. When the signal came from that blinking window of yours, I just notified the authorities—who've been suspicious of the layout for some time, by the way—and we swooped down on you like the U.S. Cavalry."

"And in the nick of time, too," Gil said, remembering. "How's Carla?"

"Great. Not a scratch on her."

Gil hesitated. "Murphy, about what happened at the airport ..."

Murphy grinned. "Forget it, Gil. You don't think a sissy punch like you have can hurt a solid Irishman, do you?"

Gil grinned back at him. "I guess not." His face clouded. "But I am in love with Carla."

"Naturally. That's the conclusion I wanted you to reach when I made up that fantastic story about me and Helen being separated. Carla's a nice girl, but she's too skinny for me. I like my women plump." He glanced at his wristwatch. "Which reminds me, I have social obligations to take care of—like getting home to a nice warm bed that'll get much warmer when I crawl into it."

"Braggart!"

"No," Murphy said seriously, "just honest. There's a young lady waiting outside to see you. Shall I send her in?"

"By all means. And I'll see you in Los Angeles."

"Right," Murphy said, and went through the door.

A moment later the door opened, and Carla came in. She was wearing a brand new blouse and skirt.

"Hi," she said. "You've been shopping."

"A girl can't run around naked all the time."

"How about special occasions?" he asked, reaching for her with his good arm.

She squirmed away playfully and held out an envelope to him. He took it from her, tore it open. There was a note inside. He read it, then carefully folded it, returned it to the envelope.

"It's from Brenda," he said. "She's out on bail and wants to forgive and forget and start all over again."

"And?" Carla prompted.

He shrugged. "Well, it's the best offer I've had so far today."

"Is that so, Gil Baxter," she exploded, waving an irate finger under his nose, "well, you listen to me ..."

"Sure," he said, grinning at her, "but I'm a sick man, so whisper it into my ear."

He reached out and grabbed the hand waggling in front of his face and pulled her onto the bed with him, where he encircled her with his good arm and held her tight.

"Gil, you shouldn't ..." she protested.

He cut off her protest by covering her lips with his own and shortly her struggles ceased and she murmured gently beneath his caress.

"What was that you were going to tell me?" he said, after awhile.

She whispered in his ear.

He laughed, pleased. "Is that a proposition or a proposal?"

"Both."

"In that case, I'll take it."

Carla rose from the bed and went to lock the door. When she returned, he reached for her again.

"Hey, wait, you're supposed to be weak from loss of blood, remember."

"That's right," he said. "Help me."

She helped him.